Not Your Lucky Day

Trentbridge Crime Series
Book Six

Lee Wood

Rollercoaster Publishing

Not Your Lucky Day

Copyright

This edition was published by Rollercoaster Publishing 2023.
 This book is a work of fiction, and, except in the case of historical fact, any resemblance to actual persons, living or dead, is purely coincidental or used with consent. Every effort has been made to obtain necessary permissions with reference to copyright material, both illustrative and quoted. We apologise for any omissions in this respect. We will be pleased to make the appropriate acknowledgements in any future edition.

Paperback ISBN: 978-1-871407-44-0
Large Print Edition: 978-1-871407-67-9

Not Your Lucky Day

Lee Wood

BRITISH CRIME WRITER

Map of Trentbridge

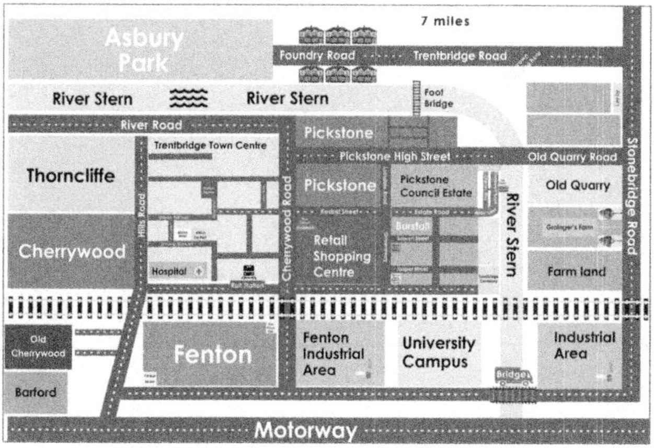

A town based in the North West of England, with a population of 260,000

ABOUT THIS BOOK

If you have read any of my previous books, you will know that one of the things I hate most is social injustice.

The Pakistani grooming gangs in the UK are real. And they have been around for at least thirty years. Rotherham, in the 1990s, was a dangerous place for young, underage girls. Especially those between the ages of eleven and fifteen.

As reports of the problems rippled outwards, you would imagine the police and social services would come to the rescue. After all, these were children. Young, innocent girls who knew nothing about the world. They needed protection from the dangers around them. However, for the first twenty years, the police and social services denied it was happening. They turned a blind eye until the national press got involved. It seems they were scared of being branded racist. As a result of their lack of action, thousands of girls suffered. Some still are! Many of them were from broken homes or had parents addicted to drink, drugs or both. They had no one else to help them. If you were one of the people who were involved and did nothing, I hope you now regret your inaction. Hang your head in shame.

This book is a work of fiction. The characters are fictional but based on the lives of many girls caught up in the atrocious incidents that happened, not only in Rotherham but also in many other towns and cities across the UK.

This is the story of one young girl's struggle to overcome the cards that life dealt her and try to make something of her life despite all the difficulties and obstacles placed in her way.

In researching this subject, I read several books that show what these girls went through. I will list them all at the back of the book. But I was especially inspired by the book written by Jayne Senior. She was the only person who took the girls seriously. At the same time, the police and social services did nothing.

The book is dedicated to Jayne and to all the young girls.

It is also dedicated to one of my music heroes: Grace Slick of the band Jefferson Airplane.

There is a song believed to be about her called "Rock & Roll Woman" by the band Buffalo Springfield. You'll understand the relevance of this as you get into the book.

This book's plot differs from the ones I have written in the past and the ones I will write in the future. But something inside of me said to write it. And if people hate it and the reviews are bad, then so be it.

ONE

February 1996

Joanna and Layla walked back from school. They were heading for the children's care home. It was where they'd been placed by the Rotherham Council Childcare Services department. Sadly, the last thing the people running the home offered to the kids was care. The only good thing to come out of their stay was that the pair had become close friends.

Turning the corner into Sandbach Road, they spotted a shiny white Mercedes taxi. Leaning against the driver's door was a young Pakistani man. He was smartly dressed in a dark blue suit with a red chequered shirt, the top two buttons undone. His dark hair was nicely styled, and he looked to be in his mid-twenties. He was casually smoking a cigarette.

"Hey, girls. How are you doing? I'm Mohammed.

"Fancy a ride? How about I take you into town? Treat you to some food and a drink." He gave them a big smile.

The pair looked at each other and started to giggle.

"We can't," said Joanna. "We have homework. And besides, the council home where we're staying is pretty strict about us going out."

"You can do the homework in my car as we drive. It's really comfortable. It's got leather seats and that. You both look, what, eighteen? Surely, you can make your own decisions."

The two giggled. "We're only thirteen," said Layla.

"Wow. You look so sophisticated. I thought you were a lot older. And you're both so beautiful. Tell you what. How about we go into town, and then I bring you back? An hour at most. Where's the harm? Come and have some fun?"

Joanna whispered in Layla's ear. "No harm if it's only an hour. What do you think? He looks well fit."

Layla whispered back. "Yeah. He does. Come on. Let's do it."

As the girls hopped into the back seats, Mohammed pressed a button on the car stereo. The track "Everybody" by The Backstreet Boys drifted from the speakers. He turned it down to a background level.

"So you both live in a children's home. What's it like?" he asked, turning his head to address them as he spoke.

"It's horrible. They try to tell us what to do. And we have to be in bed by nine o'clock," said Layla.

"Yeah. And what they feed us is crap. The woman in charge can't cook to save her life. It tastes foul," said Joanna.

"Well. The place I'm taking you to makes real food. You'll love it."

Ten minutes later, Mohammed parked outside Goodfellas restaurant by the Parkgate Shopping Village.

"Here we go, girls. The best food in town."

Between mouthfuls of food and sips of cola, Mohammed told them he lived in a large house with five bedrooms.

"In my religion, arranged marriages are quite normal. So I'd bought the house expecting to get married and start a family, and then I thought *fuck that*. I don't want to be stuck with someone I've never met. I want to have fun. Not be tied down. Know what I mean?"

The girls nodded in agreement as they tucked into the food.

Mohammed glanced at his watch.

"C'mon. We've only been half an hour. Let's go and have a look around the shopping centre."

He led them around, stopping at one of the clothes shops. "Look. Tell you what. Go in and buy yourselves some clothes. Maybe a nice top. I'll pay for them as a treat."

Mohammed strolled around the nearby shops while the girls looked along the racks.

After trying on several tops, they came over to him from the changing rooms.

"Can I have this one, please?" asked Layla, holding up a black ribbed racer vest.

"And I'd like this one, please," added Joanna, holding up a blue t-shirt with the outline image of a dog made of daisy flowers.

"No problem," said Mohammed. As they walked outside, he glanced at his watch. "I guess it's time to take you back. I was going to show you my house, but we can do that another day. What do you say?"

"Oh yes, please. We'd love that," shrilled Joanna.

Mohammed dropped the girls at the end of their road, close to the care home.

"I'll catch up with you in a day or two. Be good," he said.

"We will," replied Layla. "And thank you for the clothes."

Mohammed drove off with a big grin on his face. It had cost him thirty-two pounds for the meal and the clothes, but it would be worth every penny once he'd reeled them in.

Two days after their first meeting, they saw Mohammed as the pair walked back to the care home from school. He was parked in the same place as before, leaning against his car. When he noticed them, he dropped his cigarette and crushed it. "Hi, girls," he said. "How are the clothes?"

"They're great," said Joanna.

"Fancy coming for a ride?"

"Where did you have in mind?" enquired Layla.

"Wherever you want to go. Something to eat. Shopping. You name it."

"We'd prefer to go shopping," said Joanna.

"Okay. Tell you what. If I buy you some new clothes, how about you come back to my house and try them on? Then I can see if my money has been well spent."

The two girls looked at each other as if they could read the other one's mind.

"Yeah. Okay," they said, almost in unison.

Mohammed drove them to the Brinsworth Lane shopping centre and took them into the New Look clothing store.

Fifteen minutes later, the two girls emerged, each holding a carrier bag. They jumped in the back seat of the car.

Mohammed drove into the driveway of a large house and pulled up near the front entrance.

"Wow. Do you really live here?" enquired Layla.

"Yep. All on my own. Come on. I'll show you around."

Mohammed opened the front door, went over to the panel on the wall and switched off the alarm.

"This is the lounge," he said, showing them into a large room with two sofas and two single chairs. On the walls were various pictures. Above the couch, close to the far wall, were three blush pink pictures, the outer two with Islamic writing. The centre picture showed two pink roses. A set of similar paintings was on another wall, close to a large wall cabinet. "Wow. It's massive. Double the size of any room I've ever seen," said Layla.

"Let me show you upstairs. You can try on the clothes and then give me a fashion parade." He smiled at them.

Mohammed led them upstairs. "These are the guest bedrooms," he said, pointing to two doors on either side. He walked to the end of the hallway. "And this is the one I sleep in," he added.

He opened the door to a bedroom with a massive four-poster bed.

"It's huge," exclaimed Joanna. "I've never seen a bed that size. You could get, what, four people, at least, in it."

"It's what they call emperor size. The largest one they make," boasted Mohammed with a smile.

"I'll leave you to change into your new clothes, but be sure to come downstairs when you've changed and show me how they look."

He walked out, closing the door behind him.

The pair looked at each other. They knew what the other was thinking. Layla went first, diving onto the bed, quickly followed by Joanna. They rolled around from side to side, enjoying the softness and comfort of the luxury pocket-spring mattress.

"One day, I want a bed like this," said Layla.

"Yeah. In your dreams."

"Why not? I just need to find a bazillionaire. A handsome one. Not some old bloke, like over forty. Ugh!"

"Mohammed is Muslim. They have more than one wife. Perhaps he would marry both of us. He's pretty fit."

"Yeah. He is, but he must be about twenty-five. That's almost twice our ages. Like, both of us put together."

They giggled at the thought.

"Yeah. But when he's forty, we'll be like twenty-eight, almost thirty."

Joanna looked at Layla. "Have you ever, you know, done it with anyone?"

"No. I sort of did something with Kevin Peters. He got it out and showed it to me. But that's all. How about you?"

"I let Nathan Vickers have a feel of my tits."

They heard a voice that sounded like it was coming from the hallway. "Are you ready yet?"

Joanna called back, "Nearly. Give us a couple of minutes."

Mohammed made his way down to the kitchen. The radio was on.

We interrupt this programme for a news update.

After four years of separation, it has been announced today that the divorce of Prince Charles and Princess Diana has been finalised. It has been agreed that Diana will continue living at Kensington

Palace and be known as Diana, Princess of Wales, but not Her Royal Highness.

He turned off the radio, walked through to the lounge and sat down on one of the sofas, waiting for the girls to appear.

"Wow. You two look amazing. Let me take some photos of you." He lifted the Polaroid camera and clicked away.

"You're both so beautiful. You could be models."

Several poses later, Joanna looked over at Mohammed.

"What's the time?" she asked.

"It's six-thirty."

"We need to be going, or we'll be in trouble. We're already late for tea. There won't be anything left for us."

"I'll buy you something on the way. But you can't eat it in my car – it will make it stink."

Thirty minutes later, Mohammed dropped them off close to the care home.

He drove off at speed. He had secret cameras in several rooms, including his bedroom. He couldn't wait to watch the video and see if the girls had stripped down to their undies.

He licked his lips with anticipation. He loved to watch things almost as much as taking part.

TWO

March 1996

It had been four days since their previous *adventure* with Mohammed. Joanna and Layla were giggling, as usual. They might live in a children's home and have no family to support them, but the girls always looked at things from the positive side. So, they went through life giggling at everything. After all, it was far better than the alternative.

As they walked home from school, Mohammed was waiting for them. They hopped into the car, and he drove off, heading for his house.

Within minutes of arriving at Mohammed's, the girls had turned on the TV and settled into his lounge sofa.

"Hey, girls, try this," he said, handing each of them a glass of clear liquid.

"What is it?" asked Layla.

"It's vodka. All the top models drink it."

"Ugh. Gross," said Joanna after taking a sip.

Layla took a sip, then another. "It's not so bad."

After a couple more drinks, Mohammed said it was time to leave.

"Oh, do we have to?" asked Joanna.

"I've got to get you back, otherwise, you'll get into trouble. Look. I tell you what. Why don't you leave the home and come and stay here? I've got five bedrooms. You can stay in one."

The two girls had looked at each other and giggled. "You mean it?" asked Joanna. "You'd give us a room? What's the catch?"

"No catch. Just do some work around the house. Cleaning and tidying. That sort of stuff."

They giggled again and looked at each other.

"Why not?" said Layla. "Yeah, anything to get away from the old dragon."

As he drove them back, they chatted about when they would leave. They set a date for the following week.

Today was the day they had agreed to move into Mohammed's house.

They hadn't told anyone at the children's home. Why should they? Nobody there gave a toss about them. They probably wouldn't even notice they were gone.

As they turned the corner into Sandbach Road, Joanna and Layla started to giggle, as usual. Up ahead, Mohammed was leaning against his taxi just a few yards from the council care home. They had been waiting for this moment all day. They had been giggling and whispering during every lesson. The teachers had told them off, but they didn't care.

Before they left for school this morning, they had loaded their holdalls with as many clothes as they could cram in.

As they got close, Mohammed asked, "Hello, girls. Are you ready for the move?"

They looked at each other and, as usual, burst into a fit of giggles.

The girls placed the bags in the boot and clambered into the back seat of his shiny white Mercedes.

"Okay, girls. Here we go."

THREE

April 1996

It didn't take long for the two girls to find out what Mohammed was *really* like. They had thought he was their friend and he would look after them. Sadly, they soon found out the truth.

The first night, as they were getting ready for bed, Mohammed brought a bottle of vodka and two men up to their room. They both looked like they were in their thirties.

"Girls. These are friends of mine. I would like you to be really nice to them."

The two naïve thirteen-year-olds were about to discover the tragic cost of accepting Mohammed's offer of somewhere to stay. They would be expected to entertain a constant stream of Pakistani men who only wanted one thing. And didn't care how rough it got.

Entertaining Mohammed's "friends" became the norm. As the days and weeks passed, the girls lost another part of their innocence. The giggles dried up, replaced by tears and disillusion as their positive outlook on life started to drain away.

Every night, there were four or five men lining up to have sex with them.

Most of the men only lasted a few minutes before they'd had their "fun". Then, they would be on their way. The problem was, it meant another man was waiting in line for his turn.

The truth was, they were two innocent young girls. They should have been enjoying their childhood filled with love and laughter. Instead, they were caught in a world of abuse and evil. A place where they were gradually being groomed to think what was happening to them was normal.

Mohammed would often drive them to other places. Rooms above takeaway restaurants or scuzzy flats in various locations all across Rotherham. It was always the same: a group of men who would take turns abusing them.

It was an epidemic spreading across Rotherham. Often, they would come into contact with other girls suffering the same fate as them. Totally ignored by the authorities. Many were from broken homes. Social services knew exactly what was happening but did nothing. Instead of helping, they turned a blind eye. They didn't seem to care that hundreds of vulnerable underage girls were being lured into having sex with older men.

It seemed rather than protecting the human rights of the young underage girls, they were more concerned about the human rights of the men who used the ethnic-minority card. Often, it would start with a younger Pakistani man who would befriend a girl and tell her she was beautiful. The next step was for the men to say they were their girlfriends and get them to have sex.

Then they would be invited to a party, lured by the thought there would be music and dancing, when the reality was, they were there for the men's pleasure. Most of the men there were old enough to be their father. And most of them married with families.

A few of the new girls who didn't understand what they had gotten themselves into would scream when they realised what was about to happen. They were slapped around until they gave in.

The girls would be given drinks of vodka and then, when they were drunk, they would be taken to a bedroom, and the men would line up waiting to take their turn.

As well as the vodka, they were given drugs, like cocaine, cannabis or mephedrone, before being raped and abused. Anything to help keep them passive and easy to control.

And if they didn't go along with it, threats would be made against members of their family, or warnings of what could happen to their younger sisters. Or hints about their house being set on fire in the middle of the night, or even murder.

FOUR

1998

It had been two years since Joanna and Layla had come across Mohammed. Over that period of time, nothing had improved at the children's home. If anything, things were worse. The staff were still uncaring, and workers in social services were still useless at their jobs. So it was no surprise that many young girls had run away. The latest was a thirteen-year-old by the name of Ashley Grace McDonald.

Another young girl whose only wish was for a better future. She had been placed in the home by Rotherham council after her mother had passed away. Her father had died two years previously.

In the week since leaving the care home, she'd been sleeping rough in the garden shed of an old, abandoned house. But earlier today, builders had come in to start work, and told her to leave. They put a padlock on the shed and wouldn't even let her in to collect her stuff. *Bastards*!

She'd been standing outside Vinnie's fish and chip shop.

Wearing only a skimpy top and a thin jacket. Her teeth chattering from the cold. Anyone she saw heading inside, Ashley asked if they'd buy her some food. *After forty minutes, as she was about to give up hope, a knight in shining armour came to her rescue. Well, one in a shiny white Mercedes taxi.*

A smartly dressed, good-looking Pakistani man who looked to be in his mid-twenties.

He told her his name was Mohammed Khan.

"I-I-I'm Ash-Ashley," she replied softly, shivering.

"You're bloody freezing. Get inside the car. I'll turn the heating right up. And it's really comfortable. Got leather seats and everything."

Ashley didn't need persuading. She jumped in the passenger seat.

Mohammed handed her a small silver cup filled with a clear liquid.

"Here. Drink this. It'll warm you through."

Ashley raised the cup, took a swig, and almost choked.

He laughed as she spluttered and coughed.

"What the bloody hell was that?"

"Vodka. You'll get used to the taste. Have another." She hesitated. "Go on. It won't harm you. Take another swig."

She felt obliged to do as she was told.

"Tell you what. Go in and get two portions of fish and chips, and we'll go back to my house and eat them. It's not far."

Three minutes later, she came back and went to hand over the change from the ten-pound note he'd given her.

"Nah. You keep it. I've got plenty."

"I couldn't."

"Look, don't worry. I make good money. Take it."

Ashley stuffed the money into her pocket. "Thank you."

"Think nothing of it. I know you'd do the same for me."

Mohammed started the car and drove off.

"So how come you were asking people for food? Don't you have any money?"

"I ran away from the council care home a week ago. I took some food from the kitchen, and I've been living in a shed. But this morning, someone came and locked it. All my food was inside. And it means I haven't got anywhere to stay." "Well, you can stay at mine. I've already got two girls there with me. You might know them: Joanna and Layla. They were in the care home."

"No. I don't know them. Are they staying with you?"

"Yes. They've been with me for about two years now. The house has five bedrooms. They share one, which means there's plenty of room for you."

"Will they be there when we arrive?"

"Yes. They are a couple of years older than you, but I'm sure you'll get on well with them."

They drove on in silence.

Ashley could hardly believe her luck. An hour ago, she'd been homeless and hungry. Now she was inside a lovely warm car on her way to a house where she would find a nice warm bed. And Mohammed seemed so nice. How lucky could she be?

Ashley's eyes widened as the car pulled into the driveway of a large house.

"Wow. You live here?"

"Yep. C'mon, let's get inside before the chips go cold."

Mohammed introduced her to Joanna and Layla.

"Girls. This is Ashley. She's been living at the same care home where you were. Now she's come to join us. I'm sure you'll make her welcome. I've put her in the bedroom next to yours. We'll eat our chips, and I'll show her around and then you can have a chat."

Mohammed had sat her down and given her a few more shots of vodka. Then he explained. "I give you a free place to stay and food. In return, you do little favours for my friends."

FIVE

1998

For Ashley, every day seemed like a living nightmare. Finally, after two months of daily abuse, she couldn't stand it any longer. She needed to find a way to escape.

Leaving was impossible because the girls were never left on their own. When Mohammed went out, one of his family members was usually at the house. There were six of them. Hamza and Mazz were Mohammed's older brothers. Ahmed, Fahad, Nadeem and Umar were his cousins. They ensured the doors and windows were securely locked if one or more of them were not around. The girls were kept virtual prisoners.

There was only one man who wasn't from the same ethnic background. They called him YoYo. Ashley had overheard someone say he was a police officer. But he certainly didn't act like one. He was a regular visitor to the house and would often visit her room.

He told Ashley she was a gift from Mohammed for favours he had done. He didn't talk much, and made no mention of what the arrangement was.

She guessed it was about protection because Mohammed and his friends often boasted about their contacts in the police and local council.

Mohammed was making a lot of money from the girls and wanted to protect his investment.

One night, after the first bunch of men had finished with her, Ashley had a shower and dressed. The men were all downstairs in the lounge. She had come to recognise the Isha prayer. She waited and then crept down, avoiding the two steps that squeaked as you trod on them. She had never timed how long it took them to pray but knew she only had a short time before they finished. Then, the ones who hadn't already visited her room would come upstairs.

As she turned the front door handle, her hand was sweaty. Thankfully, it was unlocked. She knew that one of the hinges made a sound, but it could be avoided if you lifted the door slightly as you opened it. Her feet felt the concrete path outside, and she closed the door as gently as possible, still lifting it.

She was breathing hard, trying not to make any noise. As she turned to get ready to run, she saw them. Two of the men from last night. They were standing by a taxi, smiling at her as if to say, "Nice try but no luck". They moved toward her. She ran down the side passage of the house; the only thing between her and freedom was the side gate. It was always unlocked. She reached it and turned the handle. It didn't move. She tried again. But it stayed firmly in place. There was the sound of footsteps. They were right behind her now.

She turned, but even before she did, she knew what she would see. At that moment, her body surrendered to what she knew would be her fate tonight, and probably for every night to come.

SIX

1998

It had been a week since her attempt to escape. Tonight was the same as virtually every other. Mohammed had given her a few shots of vodka and then sent a string of men to her room. There had been five tonight. As Mohammed put it, she would be expected to "make them happy".

The following day, Mohammed would make sure she took a birth control pill. A few of the men were not prepared to wear a condom. One of the men, who was a regular visitor, worked in a pharmacy. He would bring fresh supplies for the girls.

Thankfully, with most of the men, the sordid act was over in less than five minutes. Some would get dressed and leave, often without a word. Others would roll over and fall asleep. A few were friendly and would chat with her. But it was just a matter of time before they were gone, and the next one would visit, and then the next. Usually, it was between four and six a night. Ashley would finally get to sleep at around two o'clock and sleep until nine.

After her first attempt to escape had been such a failure, she started to hatch her second plan. This time, she would have to be a lot smarter.

The best way was to slowly gain Mohammed's trust. It might take as much as a year, but she was determined to get away from this hellhole. One of the things she did was to be friendly after they had finished having their "fun" with her. She would look interested in what they had to say. It was better than having their sweaty bodies on top of her. Or their tongue rammed down her throat and smelling their foul breath.

Apart from the police officer called YoYo, the men were all British-Pakistani. They seemed to think they had a right to take advantage of her.

She learned who the men were and what they did. Most of them were taxi drivers. Some were shopkeepers. Others were solicitors or even doctors. A few said they were high up in the local council. One said he was in charge of the housing department and talked about the deals he did for friends.

New girls were recruited from broken homes. Often, the parents were drug addicts, and the girls had been put into care homes. Council workers seemed to turn a blind eye as taxi drivers called and took them away. The girls would be returned hours later, the worse for drink or drugs.

The men said that if any of the girls talked to the police, they would find out about it. One of the men even boasted that they were, as he put it, "untouchable". They could do whatever they wanted, and no one would do anything about it.

Ashley knew she was attractive because a lot of the men

would seek her out. Her breasts had developed, and she was starting to get curves in the right places. Many made a beeline for her and said she was the prettiest and their favourite.

Part of the reason for this was because, when they visited her, she would respond. Pretending to enjoy what they were doing made her stand out from the girls who would simply lay there and take it. It would make them think they were Allah's gift to women. And, in turn, they would tell Mohammed how good she was.

To cope with it, she would close her eyes and try to imagine they were boys of her own age. In her mind, she was doing what you did with a boyfriend instead of smelly, fat men in their forties and fifties. She had decided to do this after seeing one girl attempt to resist their advances. She had seen what had happened to her. It wasn't pretty. Not long after that, the girl disappeared.

Many of the men opened up to her, and she learned a lot about what was happening. It seemed there were hundreds of young girls in Rotherham in the same situation.

When she met Mohammed, Ashley had been thirteen, but recently, she had seen girls brought to the house who were much younger than her. He was always keen to get hold of girls aged around eleven or twelve. Then, the following day, they were gone. From what some of the men told her, such was the demand for what they termed "young, fresh meat" that they were taken from place to place to be shared around.

Ashley wondered how these men could justify what they were doing. It didn't seem to be in line with their strict religious principles. What sort of God would approve of this kind of thing?

SEVEN

Ashley had worked out that the best way to get away from Rotherham would be by train. To do that, she would need money.

Most of the men who visited her were taxi drivers. And they would usually have a large number of one-pound coins. So, for them, she would pretend she was enjoying their attention and make them last a little longer. It meant they would usually fall asleep when they had finished. This would give her a chance to go through their pockets.

She would only take loose change, two pounds at the most. And she would never take notes, just in case they noticed. This way, they hopefully wouldn't get suspicious. After all, a coin or two could easily have fallen out of their pocket. Her aim was to have two hundred pounds by the time she was ready to escape.

One of the tasks she did for Mohammed was to go into the post office and collect the road tax discs for the taxi drivers. While she went inside, he would wait in his car. She was grateful for that. It allowed her to change the coins she had stolen into twenty-pound notes.

Little by little, it seemed that Mohammed was beginning to trust her more, especially after the tests he'd set for her.

One day, he had taken her to the supermarket, pretended he had a stomach ache, and had to visit the gent's toilet. It was a test to see if she would rush out the door. Fortunately, she had overheard them discussing it the night before. Mohammed had arranged for taxi drivers to be parked in different places around the car park. That way, they would be able to stop her if she tried to make a run for it. Knowing their plan, she carried on getting the items from the list. Then, she went back and waited for him to come out, pretending she was concerned if he was alright.

He did a similar thing when she went to the post office one time. Mohammed rushed in, said he needed to pick someone up from a few streets away, and told her to wait outside until he returned. He left her there for twenty minutes. Then, he told her he had forgotten he had dropped her off and had got halfway home before he remembered.

EIGHT

1999

After three years of being trapped in the house, Joanna and Layla were surprised when Mohammed called them down to the lounge one afternoon.

"Girls. I'll come straight to the point. You're both sixteen now. My friends and I have enjoyed your company, but the truth is, they want younger girls. So, I can no longer offer you the hospitality of my house. Tonight we are going to have a special leaving party. Then tomorrow morning, I'll take you to the station and put you on a train to London. You will be free to start a new life. I have a friend down there who will give you jobs in his restaurant. I'll give you his address when I take you to the station.

"But, tonight, you need to put on a special show. A sort of..." Mohammed hesitated, trying to find the right words, then smiled. "A sort of special treat. A going-away celebration.

"I want you to dress up and make yourselves look extra

special. You will come downstairs at ten o'clock and celebrate with my friends.

"Now go up to your room. Here are the clothes I want you both to wear tonight."

The two girls made their way upstairs to the bedroom they shared. It all sounded too good to be true. Mohammed was not known for his generosity, so to pay for tickets and send them to London sounded strange. But then, they had served their purpose over the years. He'd made a small fortune from renting them out to other men. Now, the men wanted younger, innocent girls. Like they had been when they first arrived. So, now they guessed it was time for some new girls to take the abuse and be used, just as they had been on thousands of occasions.

They spent the rest of the afternoon sitting in their bedroom, discussing what they would do when they arrived in London.

They hadn't had a chance to ask Mohammed if he would give them any cash. He was always tight where money was concerned, so they thought there was little chance.

"The first thing we need to do when we get there is find a job. Not with his friend. Even if it's McDonald's or a restaurant, at least that way we'll get some food," said Joanna. "I don't want anything to do with Mohammed's friend."

"Yeah. And it will be nice to be free of these bastards," said Layla.

At eight o'clock, they started putting on their make-up. Then they put on the outfits that Mohammed had given them. They looked in the wall mirror, then turned to each other.

"What do you think?" asked Layla.

"I guess it's no surprise, knowing what this lot likes," replied Layla.

Mohammed had given them firm instructions. They were to wait until after the men had finished the Isha prayers. Then they were to go downstairs into the lounge.

He told them it would be a special party and they were the guests of honour.

Seeing their outfits, both girls had a pretty good idea of what the party would be about.

The lounge door was open, so they could hear that the prayers had finished. The girls were about to make their way downstairs. They stopped at the top to allow room for the man coming up. They both knew where he was heading - into Ashley's room. The other girl who lived, or to be more precise, was a prisoner in the house. With the prayers over, he would be the first in a long line of men that Ashley would have to "entertain" tonight.

Once he had disappeared into her bedroom, they made their way down into the lounge.

The door was open, and they could see the faces of men they knew well. The ones who visited their bedroom on a regular basis. The ones they hoped, after tonight, they would never have to see ever again.

Mohammed walked over and stood in front of the pair. He was looking them up and down. He nodded with approval.

"Yes. Yes. Perfect," he said. "Well done, girls. Let me get you both a drink."

They knew what that meant. It had been how he got

them to "perform" that first time they had arrived. Plying them with vodka and then, once they were drunk, getting them to perform sexual favours for a stream of older men.

Tonight, there were more men than usual. It was almost certain that some would leave after they'd had their fun, and others would arrive to take their place.

Layla looked at what her friend was wearing. It was very similar to her own outfit: a white blouse with a thin necktie, a school blazer, a very short black pleated skirt, knee-length socks and black high heels. Mohammed had also told them to tie their hair into pigtails and wear bright red lipstick and nail varnish.

Wearing the schoolgirl uniforms Mohammed had supplied made them look far younger than their actual age of sixteen. The men would think they were as young as twelve. To some, they might even pass for eleven. That meant the men would be licking their lips in anticipation as they queued up to have their turn. They *loved* fresh meat. The younger, the better.

Joanna noticed Hamza standing in the corner, as he often did. But tonight, he was filming everything with a camcorder instead of taking photos with his Polaroid camera.

By midnight, each girl had "entertained" seven men. A couple of them had wanted it rough. They were all Muslim, except one. Everyone called him YoYo. From what the girls had overheard in the past, he was a police officer.

Now, there were just eight men left in the room. Some had left, and a couple had probably gone upstairs to visit Ashley – she was very popular.

Finally, the men had all finished taking their turns. Joanna noticed as YoYo approached Mohammed and whispered to him. She watched him nod. Then YoYo pulled out his phone and made a call. She wondered who he was calling. Perhaps he was arranging their train tickets? But, as she watched him smile, she knew the call had nothing to do with tickets to London. She wondered what was coming next. She soon found out when three men she hadn't seen before walked into the room. These were non-Muslims, like YoYo. They were older than him: two were probably in their forties, the other in his fifties. They looked like businessmen, in their dark suits and wearing ties. Mohammed greeted them, and after a few words were exchanged, the two girls were lined up. He adjusted their schoolgirl uniforms, making them look straight and tidy.

All the time Hamza was moving around with his camcorder. Then, two of the new arrivals laid Joanna across one of the sofas so that, as she had sex with one, she was pleasuring the other.

The new arrivals were more vocal than the usual men. It seemed to excite the normally quiet Pakistani men, and they started cheering as the man having sex with Joanna became more worked up.

"Yes, yes, yes," he called out. Then he collapsed onto the floor while the other man climbed on top of Joanna and took over. He also called out as he started to climax.

YoYo and the other man had gone over to Layla, taken her to the other sofa and made her do the same with them. Hamza moved around, capturing everything on his camcorder.

After the new arrivals had finished and dressed, they briefly chatted with YoYo, shook hands, and left. Mohammed and YoYo went through to the kitchen while the girls put their clothes back on and waited to find out what would happen to them next.

When the two men re-appeared, they were each carrying a roll of plastic, which they proceeded to lay on the carpet between the sofas.

Layla looked on and seemed to be bemused. Joanna's face turned from quizzical to fearful as YoYo moved forward. He grabbed her and slapped her across the face, using the full force of his hand. She fell backwards onto the sofa. He jumped on her, placing his hands around her neck, his fingers digging into her flesh. He smiled as his grip increased, and she began to splutter, trying to cry out, but all that she could manage was a gurgling sound.

"Smile," laughed YoYo. "You're going to be the star of your own movie. Just a shame for you it's a snuff movie." He grinned, with his face contorted. His hands squeezed harder until he was sure the very last breath had left her body.

Hamza moved around to the side to get a better angle with the camcorder. At the same time, Layla grasped what was about to happen. She ran toward the door, but Mohammed was blocking her way. His older brother, Mazz, grabbed her and held her arms behind her back. Mohammed moved forward and put his hands around her neck; as he did, she brought her leg up and kneed him in the groin. He dropped to the floor like a stone and yelled out in pain. She twisted her body and escaped from Mazz's grip, making a dash toward the front door. She reached out to open it. Another couple of seconds, and she would be free. She was young and could run faster than any of these men. But as she pulled the door open, Nadeem grabbed her arm. She tried to get free, kicking and lashing out, screaming at the top of her voice, but he was too strong. Mazz came over, and the pair pulled her back into the lounge. They held her while Mohammed recovered. Layla looked across to YoYo and saw the lifeless body of her friend Joanna. Finally, Mohammed managed to get to his feet. While the two men held Layla from behind, Mohammed moved in front of the petrified girl. His face beamed as he put his hands around her throat and started to squeeze.

She continued to twist and turn, trying to kick out, fighting for her life with every fibre of her body.

Mohammed smiled when he saw the look of fear in her eyes and the tears streaming down as her face turned red and she began panting like a dog.

It was at that moment Layla knew she would never get to see the bright lights of London.

Mohammed's hands gripped around her throat until he was certain the very last breath had been extinguished from her body.

NINE

Ashley McDonald looked across at the big, fat, smelly creature lying beside her. Luckily, he had fallen asleep, snoring loudly. She carefully turned his arm to glance at his wristwatch: 1.08 a.m. It didn't seem like he would wake up for a while. She should have time to nip into the bathroom, jump in the shower and wash off the stench. This grunting pig was the latest of five men she'd had to "entertain" tonight.

As she tiptoed across the hallway, she heard what sounded like men cheering. She crept to the top of the stairs and ventured down the five steps to where the stairs bent. From there, with the door to the lounge ajar, she had a limited view.

She heard the cheers again but couldn't see where it was coming from, or what was happening. Creeping back up the stairs, she made her way along the hallway to Mohammed's bedroom.

From here, she could view everything via the secret camera he'd installed. He was a voyeur and enjoyed watching and listening just as much as he liked to take part.

She'd discovered the system while cleaning his room a few weeks ago.

Ashley turned on the TV monitor. Joanna was dressed in a schoolgirl uniform, lying across one of the sofas. She was having sex with one man while pleasuring another who was kneeling at the side. Ashley didn't recognise either of them. Neither looked Muslim. The one on top of Joanna was grunting loudly. It seemed to excite the normally quiet group of Pakistani men who were watching. They were cheering as the man became more worked up. "Yes, yes, yes," he called out, then collapsed onto the floor, allowing the man being pleasured to take over.

She noticed Layla lying on the other sofa. She recognised the man on top of her as the policeman they called YoYo. The men who were watching and cheering seemed to be the usual mix of faces: Ahmed, Mazz, Umar, Nadeem, Fahad and Mohammed.

She also noticed Hamza moving around the room, filming everything from different angles with a camcorder.

Once the men who had just had sex with the girls finished, Ashley watched as the three of them left. Then she saw Mohammed and YoYo go through to the kitchen while the girls put their clothes back on.

The two men re-appeared and were each carrying a large roll of plastic, which they proceeded to lay side by side on the carpet between the sofas.

She watched as YoYo hit Joanna, and she fell back onto the sofa. Then she gasped in horror as the abuse turned into something far more sinister. It didn't take her long to realise she was witnessing a brutal act of murder.

As she stood, hardly able to believe what had just

occurred, she watched Layla trying to escape and being caught by two of the men. Then she watched, again in disbelief, as Mohammed strangled Layla. The monitor had shown her every second of the torture.

The final thing she saw were the tears rolling down Layla's face as she gasped her last breath, and the darkness claimed her.

Ashley stood frozen to the spot, trying to take in what she had witnessed. As she gazed at the lifeless bodies of Joanna and Layla on the monitor, it was the eyes that caught her attention. Lifeless yet staring.

She put her hand over her mouth to stop herself from screaming.

Then she watched as Umar came into sight and moved one of the large sheets of plastic on the floor next to Joanna's body. Two of the other men came over and pulled Joanna onto her side, then started to wrap the plastic around her.

Another of the men, Fahad, came into sight and put parcel tape around the plastic. When they had finished, it looked more like a rolled-up carpet than a body.

Ahmed and YoYo then did the same with Layla's body and dragged it across the carpet and placed it next to Joanna. She noticed Hamza was still videoing everything.

Umar and Fahad picked up the plastic containing Joanna and carried it into the hallway. Ashley quickly turned off the monitor and tiptoed along the hallway to the top of the stairs.

She quietly crept down five steps to the bend in the stairs and glimpsed around the corner. She watched as Ahmed came into the hall from the living room and opened the front door. He stuck his head outside, looking both ways – Ashley assumed to make sure no one was around. He turned and beckoned to the others.

Ashley went back up to her bedroom. She carefully peeked through the window blind and watched as they carried the body out to one of the cars. She watched as they dumped it into the boot and closed it.

Then, she saw them carry out the second "package" and put it into the boot of a second car. Both vehicles carried the sign "Acme Taxis" on the roof.

Three men got into each vehicle, and the cars drove off.

Suddenly, from behind, she heard the big, fat pig in her bed start to rouse.

She slid back in beside him and pretended to be asleep, trying her best to ignore his foul body odour.

It was a similar stench to all of the men who visited her. Personal hygiene was obviously extremely low on their list of priorities.

As she lay on her bed and thought about how her short fifteen-year life had come to this. She could only hope the future was better. If only things could go back to when she was younger. Life until the age of ten had been wonderful. She thought about her daddy, and tears ran down her face.

She was a prisoner. Alone in the world and trapped inside a house of pure evil.

Having witnessed what happened to Joanna and Layla, she knew the chances were that she would be the next victim. She had to escape quickly. But she also had to be very careful. There would only be one chance.

She recalled the one occasion when she'd tried before,

not long after she got here. They had caught her and punished her. Escaping wouldn't be easy. The men she was up against were extremely cunning.

This time, it had to be different. She thought about her chances. If she was lucky, they were about fifty-fifty.

TEN

Tuesday, April 27, 1999

Ashley woke up and looked at the clock on the wall. It was ten o'clock. She made her way to the bathroom, took a shower and washed the filth of last night's men off her skin. As she tried to cleanse it away, she suspected it had penetrated far deeper than soap alone could reach.

She went downstairs and into the kitchen. "Good morning, Mohammed."

He didn't reply. He just looked up from the newspaper he was reading and nodded. She knew the sign. Keep quiet and try not to annoy him. She knew he had an appointment at lunchtime and would soon be going out.

Ashley took her birth control pill and kept quiet about what she had seen last night. She returned to her room, took the sheets off her bed, then went into Mohammed's bedroom and took the dirty clothes out of his laundry basket. She went downstairs to the kitchen, then. placed them in the washing machine. She wanted him to think today was just a typical day and that she would be around later.

But after what she had witnessed happen to Joanna and Layla, the sooner she got out of the house, the better.

So today was going to be the day. She hoped the trust she had built up was about to pay off. He thought she was his property. To do whatever he wanted with her. Ashley recently sensed one or two of the men growing tired of her. She realised they wanted "fresh young meat". Last month had been her birthday. Now that she was fifteen, she began to wonder how long it would be before she became too old for them.

In a place where she had been abused by every taxi driver within twenty miles, it wouldn't be easy to escape; they would all recognise her. She had to be clever.

It was the beginning of the Islamic New Year, and she knew that, with all the festivities and family commitments, the men wouldn't be coming around as much. They would be spending more time praying at the local mosque. It would hopefully give her a little more time to get away before anyone realised, she was gone.

Ashley was ready to put her plan into action. Two months ago the washing machine had broken down. The repair man couldn't come out for a couple of days. So Mohammed had got one of his family members to drive her to the launderette.

When it happened, it had given her an idea. Three weeks later, she jammed some cardboard into the lock mechanism so the door safety switch wouldn't engage. It had meant another trip to the launderette. The man who accompanied her got bored and went out to his car. Ashley had found a rear door marked 'Emergency Exit' that led to an alleyway. She would be able to use it for her escape. If she timed it right, it should give her at least twenty minutes before she was missed. On the previous occasion, as soon as she had got back from the launderette, she had removed the cardboard. That way, when the engineer came, he had reported it as an intermittent fault.

Mohammed always needed fresh clothes – for his work as a taxi driver and for prayers. He was very fussy about his clothes being clean and smelling fresh. The younger ones seemed to be particular about their hygiene. It was the older men who invariably had deplorable hygiene standards.

Her plan depended on a number of things. Between three and six in the afternoon was a busy time for the taxi drivers. So, if she called Mohammed at two-thirty and told him there was a problem with the washing machine, he would have someone take her to the launderette. She knew this would be a good time because the Dhuhr prayer time was from one-fifteen until about one-thirty. So by two o'clock, they would have finished. Then, they would have a short gap before they needed to go off to cover the school runs, airport trips, and afternoon food and grocery deliveries.

If she timed it right, it would mean that someone would drop her off at the launderette at around three. On the two previous occasions, it had taken an hour and a quarter to wash and dry the clothes. If she told the driver she wouldn't be finished much before four-fifteen, by then, she hoped to be on the train and long gone from Rotherham.

This would give her time to change clothes and leave via

the rear entrance. It was about a fifteen-minute walk to the railway station.

If she was careful, she should be able to merge into the crowd and avoid being seen by the taxi drivers who operated around the station. She had checked the train times. There was one leaving just before four o'clock.

Mohammed and everyone else had left the house. Ashley looked at the clock in the kitchen. It was twenty past one. She went upstairs and grabbed the cash she had hidden underneath the chest of drawers. The twenty-pound notes changed from the one-pound coins on her visits to the post office for Mohammed. She put a few items of underwear and a change of clothes into a carrier bag. She took it downstairs to the kitchen and hid it in the pile of clothes she planned to take to the launderette.

She walked into the lounge. It gave her the shivers to think that a few hours earlier, Joanna and Layla had been murdered right here. She noticed the camcorder sitting on the wall unit in the corner. The last thing she had seen on the monitor was Hamza aiming it at the plastic sheeting the two girls had been wrapped up in. It was bizarre. She could only imagine he wanted a memento of what had happened. Even the thought made her feel sick.

She went over to a picture on the wall and took it down to reveal Mohammed's wall safe. From seeing him open it on various occasions, she had managed to piece together the six-digit combination. She opened it and peered inside, hoping to find a large amount of cash.

But all she could see was a money belt. She opened it

and saw two twenty-pound notes, a mobile phone and a few other items. She took it and placed it around her waist. She took the twenty-pound notes from her pocket and put them into the money belt, along with the forty pounds already there.

There were four mobile phones in the safe and a book that she recognised as a copy of the Quran. She was careful not to touch it. She closed the safe and put the picture back in place, making sure it was exactly as she had found it.

At two-thirty, she called Mohammed and told him the washing machine had broken down just after she had put the clothes in. She told him she had a bunch of clothes that were wet and smelly.

He seemed to believe her, and said he would send Mazz to take her to the launderette. Fifteen minutes later she was standing just inside the front door with two large bags of dirty washing when he drove up. He came to the house and unlocked the door. She placed the bags into the boot and jumped in beside him.

The journey was made in virtual silence. Mazz wasn't a great talker. Ashley was grateful for that. When they arrived at the launderette on Doncaster Road, he helped her carry the two bags in.

"I've got to go and do a school run. How long will you be?"

"I'll be finished at quarter past four."

"Okay. I'll see you then." And with that he got into his taxi and drove off.

Ashley went over to the machine nearest to the front window. Just in case Mohammed had sent someone to check on her, they would be able to see she was using the machine. She placed the clothes into the washer, added the detergent, closed the door, pressed the wash she had chosen and sat down on the nearest chair. She glanced up at the clock on the wall: 3.18 p.m.

With her train leaving at three minutes to four and an estimated fifteen minutes to walk to the station, she needed to leave at three-thirty.

As the washer whirred away, she kept checking to see if anyone might be watching her. Looking around, she couldn't see anyone, but that didn't mean they weren't there. Mohammed was always very suspicious. She hoped the trust she had built up meant he didn't have anyone checking on her.

At three-thirty, she made her way to the back of the store, glanced around, then went into the washroom and locked the door. She changed her clothes and put on a baseball cap. As she came out of the bathroom and looked around, the two other people in the launderette were reading books.

She picked up the carrier bag with her spare clothes and made her way out of the rear entrance and along the alleyway. It came out two hundred yards along the road, next to an Asda supermarket. She crossed the road and headed toward the railway station. Every time a taxi went past, she could feel her heart rate increase. It would only take one of them to recognise her, and the game would be up, and then she would be caught.

As she crossed over along Doncaster Road, she realised a car was following her. It was Mazz. Either he had come back early, or Mohammed had got suspicious and made sure he watched her.

She started walking quicker, then noticed the alleyway next to the Furniture Warehouse. She knew it led through to Chesterton Road. She ran and turned down the alley. She looked over her shoulder and saw Mazz's car speed up. If he turned right down Shaw Road, he could get to the other end before her, and the chances were that he would catch her.

She made a decision and turned around and ran back the way she had come.

Her jacket had a red lining. She turned it inside out. Mazz would have been on his taxi's radio. It meant every driver in the area would be looking for her.

Up ahead, she saw the Asda supermarket. She rushed in and made her way to the rear. Her idea was to hide in the toilet. But, as she looked around, she noticed a taxi pull up outside. It wouldn't be long before they found her. She was about to give up when a staff member walked past and pressed the code on the door entry button marked "Staff Only". The woman walked through. As the door started to close, Ashley ran and caught it before it locked. She found herself in a large warehouse area. Over the back, there was a loading bay. She rushed over and found herself in a large yard. There was a lorry with the name Parcelforce on the side and a man standing next to the driver's door.

Ashley looked over her shoulder to check no one had followed her.

The man looked over. "Are you alright, miss?" he asked.

"I-I have people after me."

"What, the police?"

"No. Men who have abused me."

"I can give you a lift to the police station."

"I'm trying to get to the railway station to get away from them."

"Jump in the passenger seat. I'll give you a lift."

Ashley hesitated. Could she trust this stranger? Was he a friend of Mohammed's and ready to take her back to him?

"Look, young lady. I'm not going to hurt you. I promise, if you want a lift, I will take you there. No funny business."

She had little to lose. She got in.

The man started the engine.

"Thank you for helping me," said Ashley.

"I'm just guessing, but does this have anything to do with the taxi drivers?"

"How did you know?"

"My daughter had a friend who was abused by several of them. They got her drunk and gave her drugs. She's a complete mess now. And the police won't do anything about it."

Ashley wasn't sure what to say. She didn't want to tell a stranger about Joanna and Layla. She couldn't trust anyone. It might be a trap.

"I just want to get away from Rotherham."

"Okay. I understand. If I change my route around a bit, I can make my next delivery to the coffee shop at the station. Keep your head down as we pass the taxi rank. I'll drive around the back and you can avoid them."

Five minutes later, the lorry reversed up to the rear entrance of the coffee stand.

"Hang on, and I'll check the coast is clear," said the driver. After two minutes he returned. "There are a lot of taxi drivers all looking around outside. I guess the word is out and they are looking for you. Have a look behind the seat; there's a brown warehouse coat. It's my size so it should fit over your jacket. Put it on." The man looked across and smiled. He took off the pork-pie hat he was wearing. "Give me your baseball cap and scoop your hair under this."

Ashley did as the man said. He took two steps back and looked at her.

"I don't think they will recognise you in that."

"Thank you for helping me. Can you tell me the time, please."

The man looked at his watch. "It's ten to."

"I need to buy a ticket."

"Hmmm," said the man. "Tell you what, I'll come with you to the ticket office. They are less likely to be looking for two people."

While Ashley purchased her ticket, the man looked around to see if anyone was looking at them.

Ashley walked and stood next to him. "My train goes from platform four."

"I'll come with you until the train leaves."

The pair began walking over toward the platform. Suddenly the man pushed Ashley into a doorway. All her worst nightmares flashed through her mind. Either he was as bad as Mohammed, or he was an associate of his.

"Sorry about that," he whispered, "but I saw two of the taxi drivers look round. Another second, and they would have spotted us. I didn't want to run the risk. Hang on. I'll check they've gone."

Ashley sighed with relief.

The man returned. "Okay. The coast is clear. Quick."

The pair made it to the platform. The train was there.

"Probably best if we swap back hats, and you remove the coat so you don't stand out. I suggest you hide in a toilet until the train leaves." He looked at his watch. "You've got four minutes. And good luck."

"Thank you. Thank you so much. I'm so grateful for your help."

"Take care, young lady."

"And you. What's your name?"

"Ben Yaxley. What's yours?"

"Ashley. Ashley McDonald."

"Have a good life, Ashley McDonald." And with that, he walked away.

Ashley did as he suggested, found the toilet and locked herself inside until she felt the train leave the station and pick up speed.

ELEVEN

Tuesday, April 27, 1999

Ashley fidgeted around in her seat, turning her head to look up and down the aisle of the train every thirty seconds.

When she noticed a Pakistani family wandering toward her, she pulled down her baseball cap and cowered against the window until they had passed into the next carriage.

She was desperate for the journey to be over. Every minute that passed was excruciating. Whenever a person stood up, even to stretch their legs, in her mind, she pictured them as Mohammed or one of the taxi drivers.

Even when the train finally pulled into the station, the question went through her mind. Had she really escaped from the clutches of Mohammed? Or was he playing a game and giving her false hope, before he jumped out and dragged her back to the house in Rotherham?

Her mouth was dry. She licked her lips in an attempt to produce some saliva.

As the train came to a halt at the platform, Ashley heard

an announcement from the station Tannoy system. It was blasting out a message: *Trentbridge. This is Trentbridge.* It gave her a palpable sense of relief.

She strolled out of the station. At the exit, she passed the twin fifteen-foot-high concrete columns on either side. She stopped to glance around at the unfamiliar surroundings and breathe in the air. She was free, but what about Joanna and Layla? She would like to get justice for them. But if she went to the police, Mohammed would deny it. He'd lied to her and told her they had moved to London. He told her he'd taken them to the station early in the morning and put them on a train. She knew better. She knew they were still in Rotherham, their bodies buried somewhere remote in a place where they would never be found. But if she tried to tell anyone, no one would believe the word of a fifteen-year-old against Mohammed and all his influential friends. The corrupt police officer and the councillors who had been among the men to abuse her and Joanna and Layla. And what if the people she told then contacted Mohammed and revealed where she was? No. She dared not take the risk.

She made her way over the pedestrian crossing and away from the railway station, each step a mixture of fear and elation. Here she was, a fifteen-year-old girl, alone in a strange town. But at least she was free from the vile men who had viewed her as an object to abuse in any way they saw fit. Who treated her like a piece of meat.

Hopefully, this was the chance for a new life in a town far away from Rotherham.

Getting away from Mohammed had happened so fast. She hadn't had a chance to work out what she would do once she got here. All she knew was that she would need to be careful. The world could be full of men like Mohammed. Even thinking about it brought a shudder to her bones.

The train ticket had cost her twenty pounds. Her first thought was to use some of the two hundred and twenty she had left and book a hotel room. The only problem was she didn't have a suitcase. Just a carrier bag with some spare clothes and a few items of clean underwear. She didn't know if a hotel would let her stay without any luggage. A fifteen-year-old girl on her own.

No. It was better to find somewhere to sleep rough, just like she had been doing in the garden shed when she met Mohammed. Then, tomorrow, she would look for a job and find somewhere to live.

But first, she was feeling hungry. She hadn't eaten since breakfast. She looked up at the street name: Victoria Road. In the distance, was a café with the sign "Super Tasty".

Ashley walked up to the counter and glanced at the menu written on the wall behind the counter.

"Yes, love. What can I get you?"

"Er... Beans on Toast and a mug of tea, please."

The man, who looked to be in his fifties, placed the hot beverage on the counter.

"Take a seat. I'll bring it over when it's ready."

Ashley chose the two-seater table next to the window. She glanced at the headline of the newspaper left by a previous occupant.

Jill Dando Shot Dead Outside Her Home

She put it on the next chair and pulled out the dark grey Nokia 3210 phone she had stolen from Mohammed's safe. She turned it on. There were eight numbers stored. She turned the phone off and placed it back into the money belt, taking out the other items to examine them. There were two keys on a ring, a small plastic box with what looked like a tape of some description inside, and a credit card in Mohammed's name. There were the two twenty-pound notes she'd found in the belt and the money she'd put in it at the house. She took the twenty-pound notes and put half of them back into the belt. The other half, she placed into her pocket, keeping one aside, ready to pay for the meal when she had finished. She closed the zip and slipped the belt back under her clothes.

The waiter brought over her order, and Ashley tucked in. As the knife cut into the toast, she scooped a pile of beans on top and took her first mouthful; it tasted divine. She sipped on the mug of tea – with two large, heaped spoonful's of sugar. Pure nectar. It was like a celebration of freedom.

Ashley went up to the counter and paid the £3.60 with the twenty-pound note. As she did, she failed to see the two teenage boys watching her from a nearby table.

She left the café and stood in the doorway trying to decide whether to turn left or right, although it didn't really matter because she had no idea of the area.

Ashley had come from the right, so she decided to turn left and see if she could find a decent spot to doss down for the night.

Suddenly, as she glanced down at the ground, she noticed two shadows, one on each side of her, moving at the same walking pace. She was being followed. Could it be

Mohammed? Had he found her? Then she heard a rough voice from behind.

"Give us yer money, or else."

She turned around, recognising the two young boys she had seen when she was sitting in the café. "Look, I'm sleeping rough. I don't have any money."

"We saw you in the café. You paid with a twenty. You've got at least the change from that."

"Grab her, Dean," he barked to his accomplice. "So I can check her pockets."

They both looked to be teenagers and certainly more powerful than Ashley. She knew if she tried to fight back, as she had with the men in the house on occasion, it would end with her getting hit harder.

Dean moved behind Ashley and held her arms behind her back. The first thug started searching through her carrier bag. He found her items of clothes and underwear and threw them to the ground. Then he started going through her pockets and came across the cash.

"Well, well, what have we here?" He counted the notes. "A hundred quid. Maybe she's hiding some more in her bra and knickers. Why don't we have some fun with her?"

He moved his hands onto her breasts.

"I've got AIDS. I'm HIV. But be my guest if you want," said Ashley with a venomous growl and a demonic look across her face.

"Ewww. Get away from me," said Dean as he released his hands. "I'm not touching that. What a slag."

Just then two people came out of a nearby house.

"Quick. Someone is coming," said Dean. "Yeah, we dun alright," said his mate. "Let's go."

Ashley stood and watched them jumping with glee as they divided the money and disappeared down the street.

The two people walked by. They didn't seem to have noticed anything.

She was angry yet relieved at the same time. Angry with herself that she had flashed her money in the café without thinking, but relieved the people had disturbed the two boys before they'd had a chance to carry out their threat.

Ashley noticed an alleyway. She followed it to the rear of a shop. At the far end, she found what looked like a couple of commercial recycling bins and a stack of cardboard. It looked like it might make a good place to bed down.

As she finished making her cardboard bed for the night and lay down, it didn't take long before the tears came. Had it been a mistake? Perhaps it was better the devil you know. But deep down inside, she knew getting away from Mohammed had been the sensible thing to do. Hopefully, the experience she'd just gone through was down to her own stupidity, and that was a mistake she wouldn't be repeating anytime soon.

She tried to look on the bright side. At least the threat of HIV had stopped them from searching her properly; then they would have discovered the other half of the cash she had hidden. Yes, she had been stupid, but it could have been a lot worse.

Tomorrow, she would try and find a job. She wasn't bothered by what it was; she just needed a fresh start. She might be sleeping rough, but tonight was the first time in over a year she hadn't had to put up with groping hands, smelly bodies and bad breath all over her. She was grateful for that.

TWELVE

Wednesday, April 28, 1999

It was the noise of the traffic going past that had woken her. It seemed to be made louder by the sounds reverberating along the alleyway. After the initial shock of the attack, Ashley had finally managed to get a few hours of sleep. It had taken her a couple of hours to settle. She was scared by every little noise and thoughts of the two louts returning to finish what they'd started. Getting up, she brushed off her clothes, then placed all of the cardboard back where she had found it. If it was left clean and tidy, she reckoned, there wouldn't be a problem, just in case she needed to come back tonight. She took the phone from the money belt and looked at the time: 7.24 a.m.

Walking out from the alleyway, she noticed all the people going past. The only difference was they knew where they were going. Most would be on their way to work, and Ashley would love to have joined them. A job would mean money to pay for a roof over her head.

As she followed people, it seemed like everywhere she looked she kept seeing Pakistani men. As she walked along, she was sure one of them kept looking at her. Did he recognise her? Had Mohammed managed to track her down? The whole experience had made her totally paranoid.

She tried to put such thoughts to the back of her mind. Telling herself, this was a town that she had chosen at random. It was eighty miles from Rotherham. He couldn't possibly know she was here. Anyway, by now he'd probably found another girl to take her place and hopefully forgotten all about her.

But right now, her only thought was to find a job. The problem was she didn't have a clue how you went about getting one. What do you do? Just walk into a shop and ask *Do you have any jobs?*

She recalled seeing the Vacancies section in newspapers Mohammed kept in the kitchen.

And there had been the adverts about an employment agency on TV, for *Yellow Pages*. Most phone boxes had a copy along with the local phone book. She would have to use the call box anyway because the phone from the safe had run out of battery. She hadn't thought to look for a charger when she grabbed it.

She was prepared to take any job. The only problem was that she didn't have any work experience. She'd missed out on the final years of school. She could read and write, and had a flair for maths, but that was about it. Maybe she could find a job working in a shop. Serving behind a counter. She was a fast learner, so she knew she could pick things up quickly.

But before that, she needed to find somewhere she could make herself look presentable. She found a local supermarket and bought soap, a face cloth and a hairbrush. She was able to use their toilet facilities to have a wash and freshen up.

She bought a copy of the *Trentbridge Times,* found a bench in a nearby park, sat down and started to look through the job vacancies section. But the more she looked, the more she realised there were very few jobs for which she was qualified. There were a handful looking for catering assistants and care assistants. And two companies looking for cleaners. That was something she could do. Cleaning up after Mohammed and his family and friends, who always left a mess wherever they went in the house, meant she was more than qualified.

Most of the adverts gave a phone number, and she found a phone box that hadn't been vandalised. She called the number and was asked to go along for an interview.

She found their offices on Glass Street. At first, she almost walked past. The entrance was tucked between two shops. There was a glass door marked "Apex Cleaning" leading upstairs. She walked up the grubby staircase and opened a door that said "Reception".

The girl sitting behind a desk in the corner was probably only a couple of years older than Ashley. As she walked in, the girl was painting her nails. She quickly put the bottle of varnish into the top drawer of the desk.

"Hello, I've come about the cleaning job," said Ashley.

"Please take a seat, and I'll let the manager know you're here."

She picked up the phone. "There's someone here about the cleaning job."

"He'll be with you shortly," the girl informed Ashley.

Ashley looked around. The chair she was sitting on didn't match the other two in the room. The carpet had certainly seen better days. On one wall was a blue felt notice-board with several letters from satisfied customers and two certificates of excellence from a cleaning federation. So, it seemed like they did a good job for their customers, but their own offices looked in need of a good clean.

As she glanced back at the girl behind the desk, the rear office door opened. A tall, thin man of about forty, wearing a smart suit and tie, stood in the doorway.

He looked over. "Sorry to keep you waiting. Please come in."

"I see you're applying for the cleaning job. My name is David. Can I ask your name?"

"Hello, David. My name is Ashley."

He smiled at her, and it seemed genuine. "Nice to meet you, Ashley. Let me tell you about the job. One of our current employees is going on maternity leave, so we have a vacancy for an office cleaner. You'll be part of a team of three. Have you had any experience of office cleaning?"

"Er... No, sorry, I don't," she added. "But I'm a fast learner. I'm sure I could pick it up quickly. And I'm not afraid of hard work."

The man smiled. "That's what I like to hear. Someone willing to put in the effort. The hourly rate is eight pounds sixty. We supply you with a uniform, but we expect you to keep it washed and to wear it at all times."

David went on to explain the other details of the job and then reached into his desk drawer.

"You seem very keen, Ashley. If you'd like to take this form back into reception and fill in the details, then we can see about getting you started on Monday. How does that seem?"

"Yes, that sounds very good. Does this mean I've got the job?"

David laughed. "Yes, it does. Just fill out the form, and I'll pop out and see you in five minutes."

David opened the office door and led her back into the reception area. He walked back into his office and closed the door.

Ashley sat down with the form and the pen that David had given her. She smiled. Her first job. Now she could look for somewhere to live and begin her new life.

The girl at the reception desk looked busy, reading a magazine.

Ashley filled out her name. Then, as she made her way further down the form, her smile started to disappear. It asked for her date of birth, current address, bank account details and someone the company could contact as a reference.

The man had seemed kind. She had thought about telling him her current situation. But who could she trust? She'd thought Mohammed was nice. She didn't feel she could trust a man. She put the clipboard and pen down on the chair and quietly left. The girl on reception didn't look up. What she was engrossed in must be a fascinating article. As she walked the streets, wondering what to do, she noticed a board on the pavement that read "Jobs Galore Recruitment Agency". The sign had an arrow that pointed toward a doorway. Ashley took the stairs up to the first floor.

She saw a lady sitting at a desk. "Hello. I noticed your sign, and I'm looking for a job."

"There's no one available to see you at the moment. If you have a CV, I can pass it on, or I can give you an application form?"

Ashley reached forward and took the form. "Thank you."

She glanced at the form. It asked for even more details than the one at the cleaning company.

"I'll take it with me and pop back later," said Ashley as she made her way toward the exit.

Once outside, she screwed up the form and walked over to a litter bin on the street. It looked like every company would ask for the same. She was finding out the hard way that you couldn't get a job without an address. And without a job, you couldn't afford to get an address. It was a vicious circle.

By the end of the day, she had walked miles and virtually gone in a full circle. She had found herself back near the railway station. She was almost tempted to go into the station and get onto the first available train to wherever it took her. But, in the end, decided to give it a little longer. The people she had talked to when trying to get a job seemed friendly. The only bad thing that had happened to her all day, was a couple of people asking her if she wanted to buy drugs from them. She had responded by hurrying away.

All the walking had made her hungry. She'd skipped breakfast. All she'd eaten all day was an egg sandwich.

She decided to avoid the café on Victoria Road after what had happened. She couldn't afford to lose any more money. She found a place called the Potbank Café next to a museum, and made a mental note that if she needed somewhere quiet to pass a few hours, it could be worth a visit.

She'd had one bit of good luck. One of the shops she had walked past earlier was a charity shop and she'd seen a sleeping bag in the window. It cost her five pounds. It looked like it would be another night of sleeping rough, but at least she'd be warm. She just hoped the place where she slept last night still had the cardboard there.

THIRTEEN

May 1999

Following the problems with the cleaning company and the employment agency, Ashley worried about applying for a job elsewhere. She couldn't provide the paperwork they asked for or a reference. And they had asked for her bank account details, but she didn't have one. It meant they wouldn't be able to pay her. She was only fifteen, and no one had ever taught her about such things. And she was worried that if she came to the attention of the police or social services, she would be in trouble.

Things would change when she reached sixteen, but it was probably wise to keep a distance from the authorities for now.

So, getting a job was going to be a problem. And the thought of returning to Rotherham filled her with horror.

But she would starve if she didn't find a way to come up with some money soon.

She knew she was attractive, as the men in Rotherham

had always made a beeline for her room. She had attracted far more men than the other girls. She was well-developed for her age. She had curves and an advanced cleavage. They had told her she was their favourite, not that that had made her happy. Part of it was because she had tried to please them. Also, to make Mohammed think she wasn't going to run away, when the truth was, she had been thinking about it for most of the time she'd been there. Then she remembered a conversation she'd had with one of the men. Maybe it was a way for her to make some money.

One of the Pakistani taxi drivers had taken great delight in telling her about a scam his younger brother had run in Rotherham and Sheffield. He'd even shown her one of the forms. He'd laughed, said the idea was fool-proof, and boasted it was a way of making up to four hundred pounds daily.

He told Ashley that his younger brother was twenty-four but looked eighteen. His brother would find an area with a lot of small shops, business premises or offices. Then he would go into each one, holding a clipboard and an official-looking form. He would tell them that he was a student doing a five-mile sponsored run for a local charity. He would visit every shop or business in the area and ask them to sponsor him for five or ten pounds. The taxi driver had told her that it was such a small amount for a business to pay out that they wouldn't think twice about donating. He'd said that at virtually every place, his brother would walk away with the cash. Then, once he'd exhausted the businesses in that area, he would move on to a different location. He'd even boasted that his brother had gone into the local police station, and they'd had a whip-round and raised sixty pounds. As he'd told Ashley about this, he was falling about laughing.

He'd mentioned his brother had found the charity sponsor form in a book at the library. Then he had copied it, hiding the parts he didn't want to be seen by using Tippex.

Ashley didn't want to scam anyone, but she was becoming desperate. It sounded too good to be true, but what had she got to lose?

She went into the library and, after some research, found what she was looking for. A form for a charity that protects young people. She thought that was closer to the truth.

Once Ashley had doctored the form, she'd made a few copies on the library Xerox photocopier. Then bought a clip-board from a shop that had recently opened called Poundland.

At first, she wondered if she had the bottle to go through with it. But after sitting in a café with a cup of tea for half an hour, she finally plucked up the courage.

She'd spent the time in the café reviewing her sales pitch, and what she would say, especially if someone asked her an awkward question.

The first place she tried was a hairdresser. She went in and up to the counter. "Hello. I'm sorry to bother you. My name is Caroline. I'm a student at the university. I'm taking part in a five-mile run for a local charity. I wondered if you'd be able to sponsor me. It is for a good cause. Two of the local businesses have already agreed." Ashley held the clipboard toward the girl behind the counter.

This last part was a lie. She had filled out the names of two nearby shops, and in the column marked "Donations", she had put the amount of five pounds next to each name.

Ashley flashed her biggest smile at the woman.

The lady looked at her. "Yes, of course. I'd be delighted

to help you." She opened the till and pulled out a note. "There you go. Put me down for ten pounds."

"Oh. Thank you so much. That's wonderful."

Ashley couldn't believe her luck as she made her way out onto the pavement. It had actually worked. With her confidence boosted, she walked into the next shop. Three minutes later, she walked out with another ten pounds. It seemed that as each person saw what the previous business had given, they didn't want to be outdone.

By five o'clock, she had visited most of the shops along the street. She went into the Upper Crust Café and through to the back and into the washroom. She locked the door, sat on the toilet, and counted out the money on her lap. She could hardly believe it when she had totalled it up. Two hundred and eighty-five pounds.

The scam had worked precisely as the taxi driver had described. And after the apprehension of the first visit it had been much easier than she'd thought. No one had questioned her about it, although she had her story straight if they had. She'd used the name Caroline just to be on the safe side.

The next day as she visited each business, and told her story, they continued to hand over cash. It was surprising how gullible people appeared but also how willing they were to help a good cause. Virtually no one had asked questions. Running the scam was pulling Ashley in two directions. She didn't like taking money from people under false pretences, yet, on the other hand, it boosted her confidence and allowed her to survive.

By the end of the first week, she had enough money to rent a bedsit, and buy a few items to make it look nice. Nothing fancy, mind. The room was tiny. The smallest in the shared house on Beech Road, but she didn't care. It was a roof over her head. She wondered how she would have managed if she'd taken the cleaning job. There was no way she would have been able to afford to pay the deposit and rent in advance on a normal wage. How did people manage?

Each day, as she continued to visit more shops, it was lucky she had her story straight. It appeared a couple of people knew students at the university. Many wanted to chat about all sorts of things. But it was rare for anyone to refuse to make a contribution. About half of those who did were comfortable giving five pounds. The other half were more generous and gave ten pounds. She never asked for more. That seemed an amount people were comfortable to "donate".

As she wandered around, she noticed some genuine students from Trentbridge University. The thought hit her that if she was going to continue to pretend to be a student, it would be a good idea to look like one.

So, the next afternoon she caught a bus and visited the university. She wandered around to get familiar with the campus. It would come in handy if people asked questions.

She looked at what many of the students were wearing. Then made a visit to the shopping centre and bought some similar clothes. Luckily, she could afford them now.

Trying them on in the store, she had seen herself in the mirror. Her hair looked scraggy. So she decided to have it cut in a similar style to the students.

As she was sitting in the salon, waiting for the stylist, she noticed an advert in a magazine. It was a training course to become a fully qualified beautician. The cost of the course was £5,900. But at the end of it, she would gain a diploma and be a fully qualified beautician.

Over the past four weeks, Ashley had made a little over five thousand pounds. If she could continue to run the scam for a few more weeks, she would have enough to pay for the course. And by the time the course ended, she would be sixteen. Then, she could give up scamming people and find a real job.

She was thankful for the idea, but she didn't enjoy cheating people. It wasn't who she was, but the alternative didn't bear thinking about.

She had put down a deposit of two thousand pounds for the course, which started in two months, and by then she would have enough to pay the balance.

She also had one thousand pounds in cash, as an emergency fund.

Yes. Just a few more weeks and she would have the balance for the course, and enough for her to live on while she was learning. Of course, if she needed to, she could always spend a couple of days running the scam to help pay for food and rent.

Finally, things were looking good for fifteen-year-old Ashley McDonald.

Perhaps it was lucky she hadn't got the cleaning job.

FOURTEEN

Late June 1999

It was Monday morning, and this would be her fifth week of running the scam.

Ashley was in a new area, going from shop to shop. So far, she had visited nine shops, and each of them had given her a donation. She had already made seventy pounds.

The next business she walked into was an optician's. There was a man behind the counter talking to a lady who looked like a customer. Ashley stood behind the lady with her clipboard and sponsorship form.

When she noticed Ashley, the lady stopped talking to the man.

"No, you go first. I'll be here a while."

Ashley thanked the lady and went into her usual spiel. The man pressed a button on the till and took out a ten-pound note. He smiled as he handed it over.

"Best of luck with your run," he told her.

"Thank you so much. Your donation will really help to spur me on."

Just as Ashley was about to leave, the lady stepped forward.

"Excuse me. I couldn't help but hear about your sponsored run. I'm a reporter for the local newspaper. Perhaps we could do a feature on you and help raise some more money."

Ashley hesitated. This was not something she could have anticipated.

"Er, yes, of course."

"Let me have your details and the person to contact at the charity, and I'll put something together. We can get one of our photographers to come along and take some photos. I'm sure it could help you raise quite a bit of money."

What was Ashley to do? She wasn't prepared for this. She was thinking on her feet.

"My mobile was stolen. So if you give me your details, I'll give you a call later when I get a new one."

"Okay, that sounds good. What did you say the name of the person at the charity is?"

At least Ashley had been prepared for *this* question. She gave the reporter the name she had seen on their website and the real address of the charity.

"I must go. I'll give you a call later," promised Ashley, with no intention of ever doing so.

By the following day, Ashley had forgotten about the encounter and continued visiting shops and business premises in a new area.

By Friday morning, the events of Monday and the encounter with the reporter were a distant memory. The last two Fridays had been especially good days for Ashley and her charity scam, and she saw no reason why today would be any different. But all that changed as she walked past a corner shop.

The headline of the local newspaper caught her eye.

Local Charity Scam Uncovered

She didn't have to read any more to know the game was up and, with it, all her future plans and hopes.

Ashley turned around and walked back to the tiny bedsit. She took out a pen and paper and started working out her finances. With the month's deposit and one month's rent in advance, she had spent £866. She had spent another £400 on bedding, toiletries, clothes, shoes and a haircut. Plus the £2,000 she had paid as a deposit for the beauty course.

She went to bed feeling crushed. Maybe she should have played along with the reporter. But then she didn't want her photo to appear in the newspaper. Mohammed might see a copy and track her down. She knew the money she had left wouldn't last long. And with the newspaper story, she couldn't try the charity scam again. What was she to do now?

FIFTEEN

Ashley had woken up early and spent the morning sitting in her bedsit, thinking about moving from Trentbridge. Maybe she could move to another town and start running the scam there. But the beauty course seemed to offer her the way to a better life. And she'd already paid a two-thousand-pound deposit.

She was still thinking about what to do when there was a very loud knock on the front door. The way the person had knocked so hard, she was worried someone had found out she was behind the charity scam, and it was the police coming to arrest her.

She waited as she heard the footsteps inside the house. Then she heard a knock on the room at the beginning of the downstairs hallway. The house had seven bedsits and a room where the landlord, Pushta, lived. Shortly after, she heard raised voices. Then, there was a knock at her door. It seemed like the police had found her. She opened the door, full of trepidation, and stared at the two men. They didn't look like police, but they looked official.

"Are you Caroline Asher?"

Ashley had decided to use a false name to make it more difficult for Mohammed to trace her.

"Yes, that's right."

"We're from the High Court. We have an eviction notice. You have thirty minutes to get all of your belongings together and leave the house."

"But I only paid a month's rent two days ago, and I paid a month's deposit and a month's rent in advance when I moved in. I have a receipt."

"The person you paid the money to isn't the landlord. He was a tenant who rented the whole house and then converted the rooms into bedsits and rented them out without the permission of the landlord. And what's more, he hasn't paid any rent for the past five months. So a court order has been granted. I'm sorry, but that's the law. As I said, we'll give you thirty minutes, and then we have the right to call the police and have you forcibly removed."

"But where do I go? I don't have much money left. I don't know what to do. I'm on my own."

"You'll have to phone the council, although I doubt if you'll get a reply on a Saturday, but you can go there on Monday. In the meantime, I suggest you contact a family member or a friend, and go and stay with them. You must know someone?"

Ashley had thought that Pushta was the landlord. He'd told her he owned the house. Now, from what the man from the court was telling her, he had disappeared with her money and the money from the six other people who had rooms in the house.

It seemed that Pushta had gotten away with more than six thousand pounds from the seven people sharing the house. Plus, all the rent he hadn't paid for the past five months.

Perhaps this is retribution for what I've done, she thought.

Ashley had seen a bed and breakfast a few streets away. She went in and explained what had happened to the landlady and asked if she had a room for a couple of nights.

"It's twenty-eight pounds a night, in advance. I don't allow people to be in the rooms between 10 a.m. and 6 p.m. And no gentleman friends."

Ashley booked for three nights and paid the eighty-four pounds in cash. She asked for a receipt. The landlady looked rather put out at this request. She walked off, then came back with a receipt with the details of the B & B printed across the top of the paper. Now Ashley needed to rescue her things before she got locked out of her bedsit. She walked the short distance to George Street, where there was a taxi office.

Sitting in the back of the taxi with all her worldly possessions, she wondered how many more things could go wrong.

She placed all the cash she had left into the two large zippered pockets of the money belt. But her main thoughts were about how she was going to earn money.

She desperately wanted to attend the beauty course. It offered her a way to make a better future for herself. She daydreamed about running her own beauty salon one day.

She would use the three days in the B & B to decide if she should stay in Trentbridge or go somewhere else.

But if she was going to stay, there was only one thing left for her to make money. But even the thought made her feel physically sick.

SIXTEEN

July 1999

Ashley had looked in Yellow Pages and found details for a local letting agent. She told them she was a student and explained the situation with her previous room. They didn't seem to care as long as she paid a month's rent and the deposit.

After paying for a taxi from the B & B to move all her possessions, food and other expenses, she was down to five hundred pounds. That would only last about a month, and then the next rent would be due. Allowing for food meant she would then be out of money. She needed to do something, and there was only one thing she could think of.

When she had been looking for a job and bought the newspaper, she had come across an article. The newspaper headline read: *Residents Complain About Prostitutes in Trentbridge*

It was talking about the red-light district. An area called

Price Street and said the police had received eighteen complaints.

It went on to quote one of the residents, Carol Garner, aged seventy-three.

We have heard about them taking their clients into the churchyard at St John's Church.

However, local councillor Adam Dunfield added:

As far as I'm concerned, we don't have anywhere near the same problems we used to get.

Ashley decided she needed to know what was involved, so she visited the area several times to suss it out. Once in the daytime and several times at night.

The newspaper had said the girls charged punters, as the newspaper described them, fifty pounds for sex. The article stated that most girls did it to feed their drug habit. Ashley had never taken drugs. Mohammed had given her a joint to smoke, but she'd coughed so much he'd ended up falling about laughing.

She knew that Mohammed had charged the men who came to visit her, but she had no idea how much they had paid him. If she could make two hundred pounds a night and work five nights a week, it would only take her a few weeks. Then she'd have enough to pay the balance for the beauty course.

After eighteen months trapped in Mohammed's house, with five or six men a night coming into her room, a few weeks didn't seem like much time.

Especially if she concentrated on the end result.

From what she'd seen of the girls along Price Street, most of them were a lot older than her. She wasn't sure if that would work to her advantage or not.

As much as the thought disgusted her, she decided that she had no other option but to take the plunge.

She had six weeks before the course was due to start. Hopefully, that would be enough time to pay the balance and her living expenses. Then, once she got the qualifications, she would have a future. The woman running the course had told Ashley that many of her past students had found jobs working on cruise ships. They now had jobs sailing around the world while being paid for the privilege. It sounded amazing.

Maybe, just maybe, please, God, life was about to change. And, hopefully, this time for the better.

SEVENTEEN

Late July 1999

As she was about to close the door to her bedsit, Ashley turned and rushed back in. The thought of what she was about to do made her feel nauseous again – an uncomfortable feeling in the back of her throat. She went to the tap, poured a glass of water, and took a sip.

She didn't want to go but knew she had to, turning her thoughts to the beauty course and how it would change her life.

She promised herself. It would only be for a few weeks. Then, she would be able to enjoy a new life. It had to be worth it. There was no other way.

The man behind the counter at the corner shop hadn't asked her for ID when she grabbed the two miniature bottles of vodka. She took a swig. The taste made her shiver, but it helped. It was what Mohammed had always given her and the other girls so they would perform for the men. It helped to block everything out.

Ashley arrived at Price Street, where the girls stood. On the previous occasions when she had visited, she had observed them getting into punter's cars or taking them across the road into the churchyard of St John's Church. The newspaper article stated that most of the girls were heroin users, and some had pimps looking after them.

The time was seven-thirty. From what she had seen, the pimps didn't make an appearance before eleven o'clock. She would make sure she was gone before then.

Her prior visits had given her an idea of what sort of clothes to wear.

She'd chosen what she thought the men would like. An obscenely short wine-red mini skirt, a white blouse tied just below her cleavage, black hold-up stockings and a pair of black high heels. If she was going to act like a slut, she needed to dress like one. It was similar to what she'd seen the other girls wearing on her visits. Obviously, this was the sort of thing the men expected them to wear.

Within a few minutes, cars started arriving. Each slowed down so the men inside could examine the "merchandise", ready to stop if they liked what was on offer.

Within ten minutes, Ashley had turned down offers from two cars because she didn't like the look of the occupants. It was her first night, and she was feeling petrified. As she waited for the next punter, she was aware of a large Mercedes that had stopped a short distance along the road; it looked like the driver was observing her.

Like the first two cars, she turned away the driver of the third vehicle after seeing the interior. It looked like a bomb site. When the occupant had leaned across to the passenger window, she could smell the stench of his body odour. It had made her step back onto the pavement. At this rate, she was going to end up with nothing. She quickly realised that if she was going to make any money, she needed to be less fussy. Or, hope that a better class of punter would turn up. Suddenly, the Mercedes moved forward and stopped next to her.

"Excuse me, miss. But can I ask why you are standing here and why you turned those cars away?"

The man inside looked to be in his early forties, well-dressed, his brown hair threaded with a bit of grey. His face had a warm and friendly expression.

"Because they acted like pigs, and this is my first night here. Oh, and because I may be desperate, but not that desperate!"

"In that case, miss, I have an offer for you. My name is Roger Springfield. My daughter is missing, and I need someone to find her. She's a drug addict, and I don't fit into the places she goes. But you might."

"Sorry, I don't take drugs. I can't help you." Ashley started to walk away.

The man got out of the car and followed her. "I'm so sorry. I didn't mean to imply anything. I just meant that someone of her own age group might be able to go to the places where I would stand out like a sore thumb. I'm prepared to pay five hundred pounds if you can help me. You don't look like the other girls. I was hoping..."

His voice dropped off, and it looked like he was turning to go.

"If what you say is true, I would like to help you find your daughter. And I have to admit, the money would help me."

"You'll be safe with me. I promise."

"Yeah, nothing personal, but I've heard that before. Have you got fifty pounds and a pen?"

"Yes. I can do that." The man put his hand into his pocket and pulled out a note and a pen. "Here you are."

Ashley took the fifty pounds and wrote his car's registration number down on the note. Then she tore the note in half and walked over to the nearest girl.

"See this fifty-pound note. Here's half of it, with this guy's car registration number written on it. You can't use it without the serial number from the other half. I'm getting in his car. If I'm still alive tomorrow, I'll come back and give you the other half of the note. And a further fifty. Got it?"

"Yeah, sister. I hear you. Can't be too careful with these punters. No fear. I'll watch your back. Hope I see you tomorrow for both our sakes."

Ashley handed the pen back to the man as she got into the front passenger seat of the Mercedes.

"Thank you. As I said, I'm Roger. My daughter is called Trinny. Here's a photo of her. If you can help me to find her, then I'll be eternally grateful. And I promise, no funny business. All I'm interested in is finding my daughter. Since my wife left me, she's all I've got."

Ashley could see tears forming in his eyes.

"There are a couple of squats not far from here where she's gone before. The problem is, the drug dealers have lookouts, and if I tried to go into the place, by the time I got inside, it would be empty. I'm not asking you to get involved with the drugs, but you would look the part going in there. You're the right age. My daughter is only eighteen."

Ashley didn't mention she was fifteen.

If Ashley thought the first squat had been disgusting, it didn't prepare her for the second one. There were people lying on scuzzy mattresses in most of the rooms. As she walked past the bathroom, the stench almost made her sick. Goodness knows what it was like to use it. On two occasions, she looked at the people lying around. Totally stoned and zoned out. She'd seen the effects on the girls who took the drugs handed out by Mohammed and his friends, but nothing on this scale.

She saw one girl who looked like the photo the man had given her, but she couldn't see her face, as the girl was on her side, with her arm covering her face.

Ashley moved closer and touched her. She jumped back and almost fell over as the girl reached out to her. It wasn't Trinny, but she managed to get enough sense out of the junkie as she described who she was looking for.

"Yeah. I've seen her. I know where she hangs out. What's it worth?"

"What do you want?"

"Twenty. It'll cost you twenty."

Ashley looked in her bag and pulled out a note. "I've only got ten pounds."

Before Ashley could react, the girl had grabbed it.

"The Blind Pig."

"The what?"

"It's an illegal club in the basement of the tattoo parlour on Guildford Street."

"Thank you," said Ashley.

The girl started to get up.

Ashley decided to make a quick exit, making sure not to touch anything if she could help it. She was careful to avoid stepping on the syringes that covered the floor. She walked to the Mercedes and gave Roger the news. She didn't mention the money she'd had to pay out.

When they reached the address, Ashley went inside.

After the state of the squats, it was a pleasant surprise. She had never been in a pub but had seen what they looked like on TV soap programmes. The lighting here was subdued, but otherwise, it looked much the same.

Twenty minutes later, she walked outside with the attractive girl from the photo alongside her. They made their way over to the Mercedes.

"Trinny. Thank goodness. I've been worried stiff about you."

The girl looked down at the ground, not saying a word.

Ashley answered for her. "Trinny has asked me to ask you if it is alright if I stay with her at your house for a couple of days. She says she's sorry to hurt you and loves you, but she's a bit messed up at the moment and doesn't want another argument with you." "Yes, of course. That would be wonderful. We have a spare room. It's right next to Trinny's. You're welcome to stay in there."

EIGHTEEN

Late July 1999

Ashley sat in the back seat with Trinny, who remained silent during the ten-minute journey. The only words she had spoken since getting in the car was a quiet "Thank you".

Roger drove them to a large house in Cherrywood, the smartest part of town. As they approached, the two metal front gates attached to the square brick pillars began to open as if by magic. Roger drove along the short driveway and up to the front of the house. The car stopped gently outside the large, wide door. There was a porch surrounded by slim Georgian pillars on each side.

Ashley had never seen such a beautiful house this close up.

As they walked into the hallway, Ashley asked if she could use the toilet. Roger pointed to a door on the left.

She closed the door behind her as the light came on automatically. This downstairs cloakroom was twice the size of the main bathroom in any house she had ever seen, and it didn't have a bath or shower. Everything was pure white, including the marble tiles that covered the wall.

Once she came back into the hallway, Trinny was waiting.

"Let me take you up to your bedroom. It's the room next to mine."

As they walked into her new bedroom, Ashley gave out a gasp. Like the downstairs cloakroom, it was at least twice the size of any bedroom she had ever seen. She stared at the bed; it looked massive. Not as large as the one in Mohammed's bedroom, but it seemed larger than the one she had slept in.

"It's a king-size bed," said Trinny as if reading Ashley's thoughts. "We're about the same size. I can let you have some of my clothes."

"I've never seen anything like this," said Ashley. "Are you and your dad the only ones who live here?"

"Yes, my mum moved out three years ago. Now it's just Dad and me. Oh, and Barney, my cat. He's probably out right now, but he'll come back later when he's hungry." She crossed her arms and sighed. "Dad tries his best, but he doesn't understand. If you don't have anywhere else to be, I'd love it if you stayed."

Ashley thought, with all of this, I'm not sure I do either. Why would you turn to drugs when you have a home like this?

Just then, there was a light tap at the door.

"Hello, can I come in?"

Trinny moved from the door and stood behind Ashley, seeming to be hiding from her dad.

Ashley noticed and spoke.

"Yes, of course, please come in."

"Just checking you're alright and have everything you need?"

"Yes, thank you," said Ashley.

"Trinny, would you like a cup of hot chocolate, some Ovaltine, or maybe almond milk or just some water?"

Trinny nodded her head and then looked down. "No thanks, Dad," she said, almost in a whisper, then turned away.

Roger looked disappointed but said nothing.

"How about you, Ashley?"

"My mum used to make me Ovaltine when I was young. That would be lovely."

"I'm going to my room to crash," said Trinny. "I'll see you in the morning."

Ashley followed Roger downstairs into the kitchen. She watched as he went to a wall cupboard, pulled out a jar and two mugs and placed them both next to the kettle. He pressed the ON button. "Here's the money I promised you," said Roger, handing over a white envelope. "I know I've already given you fifty pounds, but you'll find the full five hundred there."

"Thank you. And thank you for allowing me to stay. I'll move out tomorrow."

"Oh no. Please don't go. Trinny needs someone, and it looks like she's really taken to you. Please stay as long as you want. I mean it. We're not exactly short of space here. And besides," – he began to smile – "you haven't met Barney yet."

"Oh yes, I must meet Barney. Trin was telling me all about him."

"Trin. That's nice. That's what my ex-wife always calls her."

"Trin told me she moved out."

"Yes, three years ago. She was my life, but it turns out, apparently, I wasn't hers. She found a younger model and moved in with him. We got divorced last year. But they seem to be making a go of it, so I'm pleased for her. But I don't think the situation helped Trinny, and I suspect it's the reason she turned to drugs, but I don't really know. She never talks to me about it. Perhaps you can get through to her more than I can?"

"I'll certainly try."

The kettle boiled, and Roger went to the fridge and got out the milk. He took the two mugs and placed two heaped teaspoons of Ovaltine in each. He half-filled the mugs with the hot water and stirred them around, then slowly topped them up with the milk.

"I find it tastes better if you add milk as well. See what you think. Mind, it's not too hot."

Ashley picked up the mug, blew on the top to cool it, and then took a sip.

"Mmmm. That's delicious."

After they had both finished their drinks, Roger placed the two mugs in the sink.

"Just get up at whatever time you want in the morning, but please don't open any of the outside doors until I'm up and have turned off the alarm system."

"Oh, okay. Can you tell me where the upstairs bathroom is, please?"

"You have your own en-suite with your bedroom."

"My own what?"

"Your own private bathroom. It's part of your bedroom. One door is the bathroom, and the other is the cupboard for clothes."

Ashley admired the chandelier overhanging the downstairs hallway as she walked up the stairs. She crossed the landing and went into her room.

She heard Roger setting the alarm as it buzzed and then stopped. She closed her door. Trin had left some clothes on the chair at the end of the bed. They looked expensive.

Ashley opened the door that looked like it might be the en-suite. It was, and there, on the shelf above the sink, was a toothbrush still in its wrapper, toothpaste, and some moisturising cream. Just to the side were two of the fluffiest white towels she had ever touched.

Within five minutes, she had climbed into the king-size bed and rested her head on the soft pillow, and, in seconds, she was fast asleep. For the first time in years, she felt safe. It was a lovely feeling, but she wasn't sure how long it would last.

NINETEEN

August 1999

It had been two weeks since Ashley had moved in with Roger and Trinny. They both seemed happy to have her stay. And as far as Ashley could tell, Trinny showed no signs of taking drugs.

After taking some time to settle into the security of her new surroundings and enjoying a comfortable bed, Ashley decided it was time to move out. She thought it was the best thing to do before they got fed up with her.

Then there was the beauty course, which was due to start in the next couple of weeks. She needed to speak with the woman running it and explain her financial situation. Maybe she would allow Ashley to attend the next course?

It would mean she would have to go back and stand on Price Street to get the money together. But at least, with the five hundred pounds from Roger, she had enough to pay the rent on her bedsit for another month. And if she was careful, she could afford to buy some food. She found him standing in the kitchen.

"Roger. I want to thank you for giving me somewhere to stay. It's been wonderful, but I think it's time for me to leave."

"Do you have plans or somewhere to be?"

"Er, not really. I just think you don't need me anymore."

"Well. Trinny spoke with me the other day. She absolutely loves having you around. You can see the way she's perked up since you moved in. She said that she'd really like it if you moved in on a permanent basis. And I agree with her.

"Not only have you helped Trinny, but I've loved having you around. I'm not sure why you were at the place I found you, and it's none of my business, but I can see you are a decent person. Trinny and I would love you to be here. So what do you say?"

"Thank you, Roger. Thank you so much. I'd love to stay here, not because of the lovely house but because you both have been so kind to me. It's been a long time since I've felt secure. I truly appreciate your faith in me."

"That's settled then. We'll say no more."

Ashley called the letting agents and gave notice on the bedsit. The next day, Roger drove her over and helped her to collect all her things.

It had been a month since Ashley had moved in. She had already been helping around the house but decided it was time to do more. She started by getting up early, going down to the kitchen, and preparing breakfast for Roger, who, she knew, would leave for work at eight. She set up the orange juice and the selection of cereals on the table. She'd finally got the hang of using the toaster without burning anything. And the kitchen had one of the newfangled coffee maker machines. After numerous attempts, Ashley had just about mastered how to operate it. Well, in as much as the coffee that came out of it now had finally stopped tasting like dishwater. "Good morning. What have we here then?"

"I thought I would make myself useful. I've made breakfast. I hope you like it."

"That looks good. You didn't need to do that."

"I'm staying here, and you've been so kind. I need to do something to help."

Just then, Trinny walked in.

"Dad. I've had a call from Mum. She and her boyfriend are going to Florida, and she's asked me to go with them. Is it okay?"

"That's fine by me. It will do you good to spend some time with her."

"Can Ashley stay here with you?"

"Yes, of course, she can."

"Is that alright with you, Ash?"

"If I'm going to stay here, I think it's time I tried to get a job and started to pay my way. The only problem is I'm still fifteen. I'm not sure who would employ me."

"Look. I'll tell you what," said Roger, "why don't you come and work for me? I need someone to do office work, and you can come and try it for a few days. If you don't enjoy it, then you can find a job somewhere else."

"What would I be doing?"

"My office manager has been off ill for the past week.

The way you've organised the house while you've been here, I need someone to do the same thing at the office."

"I don't have any experience with office work, but I'd really like to give it a go."

The following week, Roger received a phone call from his office manager.

"Roger. The reason that I've been off ill is because I'm pregnant. The doctor has told me to take things easy until the baby is born. So, I'm sorry, but I won't be coming back to work. I hope you understand."

"Oh, Emma. That's fantastic news that you're expecting. I'm over the moon for you. Don't worry. It won't be easy, but somehow, we'll cope without you. You make sure you take it easy. And let me know if you need anything."

"Thank you, Roger. That's a great relief."

Roger called the florist and arranged to send a large flower bouquet to Emma's home.

Two weeks later, Ashley was sitting behind her office desk when Roger returned from a meeting.

"Roger, the order you asked me to confirm with Beak Street Glass for those windows. I realise I don't know much about them, but I had some spare time. So I looked online and found a company that offers the same ones, and the price is thirty-five pounds per window lower. I took the liberty of sending them the specifications, and they have confirmed they are the same."

Roger looked over at the website Ashley had on her screen.

"That's amazing. You have just saved me over four thousand pounds. I'm proud of you. You're really getting the hang of things around here."

Roger was a property developer. He built small upmarket estates of houses to a high standard – usually between four and six houses.

"Roger, what I don't understand is why the houses you build are so expensive. Surely, if you built lower-cost ones, more people would be able to afford them."

"Actually, the opposite is true," Roger explained. "It's far easier to sell one house for half a million than try to sell five houses at a hundred thousand pounds each, just like cars. The man who sells second-hand old bangers probably drives a second-hand car. The man who sells Bentleys drives a Bentley. Always remember, people with money always have money to buy the things they want. Sadly, people on lower incomes can't afford the things they want."

Ashley listened intently, taking in the advice being offered. She was keen to learn and excited at the chance to work with someone who was prepared to give her the opportunity.

Perhaps, finally, with Roger, she had found a decent and honest man. A man she could rely on. But, based on past experience, she would still need to be careful.

She had learned to her cost that most men are not to be trusted.

TWENTY

July 2000

It had been a year since Ashley moved into the house. Trinny had no interest in working with her father. On the other hand, Ashley was really enjoying it. Besides running the office, she was now going out with him to onsite visits. She was learning more and more about the secrets of the building trade. Roger showed her the way houses were constructed from the ground up. She was learning how to deal with the people involved at every level. From the architects to the tradespeople. She saw how the foundations were laid, the drainage systems, the utilities and all aspects from the groundworks to the roof. Coming into contact with bricklayers, plasterers, painters, electricians, plumbers. Even the men who drove and delivered the concrete and all the other materials. She learned what snagging is and how to check it was all completed. She was even dealing with the people from the planning department.

Roger showed her how some of the workers tried to cut

corners. How to watch out for the ones who tried to steal supplies to sell offsite. Every day was different, and she was taking it all in.

However, her favourite part was when the houses had been completed. Roger allowed her to choose the furnishings for the show homes. She was dealing with every single item. From the carpets all the way through to the kitchen gadgets. But she enjoyed the small details the most, from the feng shui layout of a room to which handles to put on the bathroom doors. Every tiny detail was essential to her. She seemed to have a natural flair for such things.

And Roger had told her the feedback from the selling agents confirmed she was doing a great job. They had commented on how much more saleable the houses were. The furnishings appealed to the ladies who came to view the properties. They, in turn, would persuade their husbands that this was more than a house. This was their new home.

Roger had seen the way Ashley was developing in other ways. She was more confident in her manner. He noticed how she spent her evenings educating herself. Buying management courses and books.

She was coming into work looking more like a manager. It was evident that Trinny had taught her about fashion. And if there was something his daughter was very good at, it was make-up, clothes and shoes.

He'd even noticed that Ashley was taking elocution lessons with a voice coach and had enrolled on a book-keeping course. For all of this, Ashley didn't ask him for a penny. She was paying for everything from the salary he was paying her. She was becoming a real asset, not only in his business but also within the household.

The friendship between his daughter and Ashley was obvious. They would go out together for an evening, laughing and joking. They would go on shopping trips together and come back three hours later with bags from a variety of stores. And he could see Ashley was being sensible, which was more than his daughter was. He noticed on some occasions when they returned home after a night out. Trinny would be the worse for drink, but Ashley was always sober and helped Trinny up to her room.

Even though she was younger, Ashley acted like a protective older sister. It seemed the days of Trinny's drug-taking were a thing of the past. It was almost as if he had two daughters.

One evening, as Roger was in the lounge watching TV, he noticed Trinny leaving the house without Ashley. He looked concerned as she got into a car he had never seen before. The first thought to cross his mind was that she was back on drugs. He went up to Ashley's room and tapped on the door.

"Sorry to bother you. I noticed Trinny going out in a strange car, and I wondered if you knew—"

"Oh, don't worry, Roger. She has a date. She met a really nice guy the other day. He's taking her to a restaurant, that's all."

Relief spread across his face.

"So you've met him?"

"Yes. He works for a travel agent. We went in to look at holidays, and they got chatting and seemed to hit it off. He seems really nice and sensible."

Finally, it looked like his nineteen-year-old daughter was

doing normal everyday things. With Ashley around, everything seemed to be under control.

After the rollercoaster ride that he'd been through with Trinny and the drugs, maybe the dark days were behind them, and they could move on.

Wouldn't that be wonderful, he thought.

TWENTY-ONE

August 2002

Trinny's boyfriend was called Gary Vickers. The couple were out celebrating their second anniversary together. The best restaurant in town was The Olive Branch. The food and service were consistently superb, and Gary hadn't mentioned anything, but he had a special surprise in store.

After the main course, as they were waiting for the dessert, suddenly Gary went down on one knee. Trinny gasped as he brought out a small red box. He opened it for her to see the sparkling engagement ring he had purchased two weeks before. "Oh my God, oh my God. Yes. Yes, I'll marry you." She flung her arms around him. The waiter had seen it before and hung back, waiting for her to enjoy the moment. As Gary and Trinny took selfies, he figured they wouldn't mind if the food took an extra minute or two.

After the meal, Gary drove Trinny home. He didn't want to go out for a drink as he had already drunk two glasses of champagne and didn't want to be over the drink-drive limit.

Trinny rushed into the house, screaming at the top of her voice. Roger thought something must be wrong, but Ashley had seen the couple together and the signs Gary had been giving out over the last few days; she had an idea of what to expect.

When Trinny told her father what had happened and proudly showed him the ring, he gave her the biggest smile she had seen on his face for years.

February 2003

In the six months since their engagement, Trinny and Gary had been looking at dates for their wedding. They had provisionally booked the reception to be held at the Albion Hotel on Shaw Street. To celebrate, tonight they were going out to a club for a few drinks.

It was just after midnight as Trinny and Gary left the Crocodile Club and began to walk over to the taxi rank. Gary noticed a gang of four men fighting with another man. He was on the ground trying to protect himself from the kicking.

Instinctively, Gary rushed over to help.

"Hey, stop that. Leave him alone. He's had enough."

"What the fuck has it got to do with you?" bellowed one of the gang members.

"You've had your fun; now leave him alone."

"Yeah, we've had our fun with him, but not you."

The thug, who appeared to be the leader, tried to hit Gary in the face.

Gary saw it coming and swerved out of the way. As he

did, the other three thugs ran over and grabbed him. The leader came forward and hit Gary in the stomach.

"Now we'll have fun with you." He laughed.

The other people hanging around the square just walked past. No one bothered to try and stop it or come to his aid except Trinny.

"Leave him alone, or I'm calling the police," she screamed.

The leader looked at her with an icy-cold stare. She could see his eyes, and she could see they weren't capable of showing mercy.

"By the time those pussies arrive, we'll be long gone, darling."

The four went back to kicking Gary. To Trinny, it seemed to go on for hours, but it was just a couple of minutes.

Trinny pulled out the mobile phone her dad had bought for her and dialled 999.

Once satisfied with their handiwork, the thugs swaggered off as if they had just given a rock band performance.

When the ambulance arrived after ten minutes, Gary still hadn't moved. He lay on his side with blood all over his face and around his body.

Trinny was in tears, sitting on a nearby wall, being comforted by one of the female police officers.

"Did anyone see what happened?" asked the male police officer to the gathered crowd.

No one said a word.

He tried again. "Someone must have seen something. A description of who did this. How many? Which way did they go? Surely one of you saw something?"

His plea went unanswered.

The ambulance crew gently lifted the stretcher with Gary on it into the back of their vehicle.

"Can I go with Gary to the hospital?" asked Trinny.

"Yes, of course, you can. We'll get a statement from you later. Don't worry. He's in safe hands now. I'm sure he'll recover from this."

The ambulance sped off with the lights flashing and the siren blaring until they reached the hospital.

It had been four days since the vicious attack on Gary. He was still on a life-support machine with no sign of brain activity. The doctors were not very hopeful.

Mr and Mrs Vickers, Gary's parents, had travelled from Sheffield. They had met Trinny on two previous occasions and got on extremely well.

The newspapers reported the police had arrested four suspects. It went on to say they had all been released on bail pending further investigations.

Trinny had been at the hospital since Gary was brought in, sleeping in a chair by his bedside.

Finally, her father had persuaded her she couldn't do any more, and the doctor confirmed it.

"You can't do anything here. Please leave it to us. Go home and get some rest. I will call you if there is any news. It could be days before we see anything change."

Two days later, the phone rang as Trinny and her father sat around, not knowing what to do.

"Hello, Mr Springfield. I'm the consultant caring for Gary Vickers. We've spoken with Gary's parents. I'm afraid there is no chance of him making any kind of recovery. They have agreed for us to turn off his life-support. They have asked if Trinny would like to come and say goodbye before we do?"

"Thank you, doctor. I'll pass on the news and see what she wants to do."

Roger put the phone down and turned to his daughter.

"What did he say, Daddy? Is Gary starting to come around?"

"I'm so sorry, princess. They have done all they can. His parents have asked if you want to say goodbye before the doctors turn off his life-support. He's not coming back. I'm so very sorry."

Trinny screamed at the top of her voice. Ashley came running down from her room.

"What is it? What's hap—" Suddenly she knew.

She rushed over and cuddled Trinny.

"I'm so very sorry. It's not fair. It's really not fair."

TWENTY-TWO

March 2003

After Gary's funeral, Trinny hardly ventured out of her room. Roger told her that his parents had decided to donate his organs to give other people the chance of a better life. They said it would help them to think of Gary as still being around.

Ashley promised Roger she would keep an eye on Trinny as much as possible. The pair agreed that someone should be with her at all times. They changed their working routine, so one was always at home.

Trinny refused to come out of her room. Ashley left food by her door, then sat on the floor outside and talked to her through the closed door – sometimes sitting there for as long as two hours. Trinny never replied or ventured out to take the food when anyone was around. It looked like she nibbled the food but wasn't eating large amounts.

The doorbell rang. Ashley rubbed her eyes and looked at the clock by her bed. It was four o'clock in the morning. She made her way downstairs and went to switch off the alarm. But found it had already been turned off. She knew she had set it correctly last night and wondered how it was off. She opened the front door. Standing on the porchway were two uniformed police officers. A man and a woman. Her heart froze.

"We know it's the middle of the night, but we need to speak with Mr Roger Springfield, please."

As they were talking, Roger came downstairs, tying his dressing gown as he did, and joined her at the door.

"Mr Springfield?"

"Yes, that's right. Has there been a break-in?"

"No, sir. Can we come in?"

"Yes, sorry. Of course."

"It's about your daughter, sir. Is her name Trinny Springfield?

"Yes, it is," Roger replied nervously.

"She's upstairs in bed. I can get her if you need to speak with her."

"I'll go, Roger. You stay here."

After a minute, Ashley came rushing down. "She's not there. Her bed's not been slept in."

The policeman turned to Roger. "I feared that would be the case. I'm very sorry, sir, but a young lady has been found down an alleyway on Guildford Street. From what we found in her pockets; it appears she took a fatal drug overdose. She left a note giving this address. It says she is sorry, but she can't cope anymore. That she's gone to be with Gary. It also says that she loves you."

Roger's face turned white. He just stood there, his mouth half-open, staring at the two officers.

"Are you related to Trinny, miss?"

"Eh, no. I'm a friend but not related."

The policeman looked at Roger, still standing and saying nothing.

He addressed Ashley.

"Perhaps if you have some alcohol, I suggest pouring a glass for the gentleman."

Ashley went off and came back with a large glass of Roger's favourite whiskey.

"Here, Roger. Drink this."

The police officers stayed for over half an hour.

Roger thanked them and walked upstairs to his room, leaving Ashley to show them out. As she walked to her bedroom, she could hear him sobbing. She wished with all her heart there was something she could say or do, but she knew there was nothing.

It had been three weeks since Trinny's funeral. Ashley had been covering the office and dealing with everything as best she could. Today, Roger came into the office for the first time.

He looked at Ashley.

"I heard from the police this morning. They say they don't have enough evidence to convict the gang without Trinny to identify them. No one else has come forward. Not a single person said they saw what happened. They are going to get away with it. God help me, if I had a gun, I'd—"

"Please, Roger. Don't talk like that. It's not what Trinny

would have wanted. She was a sensitive soul. A lovely human being. She and Gary just happened to be in the wrong place at the wrong time. Keep your memories of her as she was. As you knew her before the problems when she was happy about getting married. I miss her too. She's still with you. With us."

He sat down at his desk. He said nothing as if he was still taking in what he had just heard.

"Roger, there are some things I didn't want to deal with without you. I understand it's hard, but the best thing we can do is concentrate on work. You know I miss her as well."

Ashley moved towards the door. "I'll make us both a cup of coffee and then we'll go through everything that needs your attention."

After a long day at the office, they locked up and went to Roger's car, ready to get home. Ashley took the wheel. She had recently been taking driving lessons and had passed her test.

After a light meal, they both sat in the lounge. No TV or noise.

Roger walked into the kitchen. After a couple of minutes he came back with two hot beverages. He passed one to Ashley, then sat down in his chair.

"Ashley. Can I ask you something?"

"Yes, of course."

"You've never said anything, and before now, I've never wanted to ask, but I wondered how you came to end up where I found you that night. If you don't want to tell me, that's fine, but it's just you and me now, and I'd love to know more about you. You never talk about your family or anything."

"Then perhaps it's time I explained."

"I'm sorry. I shouldn't have brought up the subject. You don't have to say anything if it's too painful."

"No, Roger. After everything you have done for me, I think it's only fair that I tell you why meeting you that night is probably the best thing that's happened in my life."

She cleared her throat before launching into her sordid tale.

"I was born and lived in Rotherham. I can recall when I was young when times were happy. For my eighth birthday, my daddy took me and seven friends from school to a fast-food restaurant. He'd booked a whole section of the place for us, with lots of food, drink, and cake. Afterwards, there was a clown and a man who did magic tricks. The place was filled with balloons and banners saying 'Happy Birthday, Ashley'. And when my friend's parents came to collect them, they all went home with a bag filled with goodies. And Daddy had hired a video camera and filmed the party. He had it transferred onto videos, and a couple of days later, he played it on our television. He also had copies made and gave them to all my friends' parents. At school over the next few days, they all said they had loved watching it.

"My daddy was lovely. He'd often pick me up after school and take me to the local park. I'd play on the swings and slides with a few friends.

"He was always taking me and Mum to places. Day trips to the seaside and zoos and amusement parks. Even on the caravan holidays, we found plenty of things to do, rain or shine."

Ashley looked down at her feet. "But things began to change shortly after my tenth birthday.

"The happiness and laughter between my mummy and daddy turned to shouting and screaming. One day I came home from school and heard Daddy saying Mummy was a slut. At the time, I wasn't sure what that meant.

"Now I know it was about the person Mummy told me to call Uncle Harry. He used to come to the house when Daddy was at work.

"One day, I came home from school, and Mummy sat me down and told me that Daddy had gone away and wouldn't be back. She explained that he had a job a long way away.

"But the following day, from the gossip and snide remarks from older girls at school, I learned he'd been killed in a car accident. I was eleven at the time.

"I looked back at my previous birthday and remembered when Daddy came in with a large present. It was my first bike, and he taught me how to ride – running up and down the road with him hanging on to the back of the saddle and guiding me. Finally, one day, as I was riding, I looked around, and he wasn't holding on. I nearly fell off, but he saved me."

Ashley pulled a tissue from her pocket and wiped her eyes.

"I miss my daddy," she said and burst into tears.

Roger leaned forward and hugged her.

"I'm so sorry I made you bring it up," he said.

"That's alright. It was just the thought of my dad. You'd have liked him."

"Yes, I'm sure I would."

Ashley continued.

"My mum forgot my twelfth birthday. Then, for the following few months, I watched her slowly crumble. The kitchen was filthy. She wouldn't leave the house. Not even to go shopping. She couldn't cope. I guess the school contacted social services because a lady visited. She said she would come back the next week, but we never saw her again. Then another lady came after about a month. Like the first one, we never saw her again.

"When I went to school the following morning, there was a lady from social services waiting outside the classroom. A new one. She explained that my mum wasn't feeling well and would have to go into hospital to make her better. I was placed in a children's care home.

"I'd been there for three months when a lady from social services turned up and told me abruptly that my mother had died.

"She didn't even tell me how, and I was in shock and forgot to ask. At the funeral, there was only me and a social worker.

"It took a long time before I would even talk to anyone. Nobody told me what had happened or tried to offer any words of comfort. I was just left to get on with it.

"The care home was a horrible place. That's when I started not bothering about school or anything else. In the evenings, I began to stay out of the home. I started walking around the town centre and only went back at ten o'clock. By then, I had just turned thirteen.

"Then I found an empty house. It was locked, but the garden shed was large. I took a blanket and some food, ran away, and slept in the shed.

"After four days, some workmen came and put a padlock on the shed, so I stood outside a fish and chip shop, asking people if they would buy me food.

"That's when I met Mohammed.

"It was his smile that got me: big and broad. He stood there leaning against his white Mercedes taxi. Smoking a cigarette. He offered me one. I'd tried a couple in the past but didn't really like it. But I guess I wanted to look older than thirteen.

"He seemed like someone I could trust. He looked cool. I was cold, and he said I could sit inside his car. It was nice, with soft seats, the radio playing the type of music I liked. We talked for ages. He was the first person I had met who really understood me.

"He told me he had a spare room, and I could stay there. I'd be safe. He never used the room, so it wasn't a problem. He said I could stay there for as long as I wanted. He said it wasn't a problem that I had no money. He'd look after me.

"We arrived at his house. It was big. He took me inside.

"My first night in a comfortable bed. I got in and fell asleep quite quickly. Suddenly, someone turned on the light. Mohammed stood in the doorway with two other men. He said they were his friends and, like me, had nowhere to stay tonight. They had missed the bus. He said the bed was big enough for them as well as me. Looking back, how could I have been that stupid?

"The two men got into bed with me and began to feel every part of my body with their hands. I was young and didn't really understand. Mohammed told me it was an act of our friendship. He passed me a glass. I didn't know then, but it was full of vodka. I drank some. It didn't taste very good. Then he said if I did the things the men wanted, it showed he was my friend. So, I let them.

"It was the same every night. There were so many of them. I thought he was going to take care of me. I wanted to be his friend. I wanted to please him. To make him like me. So, I did what they asked."

She glanced up at Roger.

"Looking back, I wonder how I could have been so naïve. But I was only thirteen and had no idea what to do.

"Eventually, after about eighteen months, I managed to escape and caught a train to Trentbridge. Because I was fifteen, I couldn't find a job. I needed money to pay for a beauty course, and the only way I knew to make money was to sell myself. And that's the night you found me."

She didn't tell Roger about the murder of Joanna and Layla. That would remain a memory for the rest of her life. Telling Roger would only upset him, and that was the last thing she would ever do. She often wondered what her life would be like without him. Certainly nothing like as happy as it had been since the day that he found her on Price Street.

Roger went over and sat next to Ashley and cuddled her.

"You're safe now, Ashley. We're family, and I'm here to look after you."

The pair sat in silence.

TWENTY-THREE

February 2005

Ashley was busy preparing the evening meal when Roger walked through from the lounge, opening a letter.

"The food is ready if you want to set the table."

Roger looked up from reading.

"What. Oh, yes, that's fine." He seemed to be distracted.

As they sat down to eat, Roger looked across the table.

"I got a letter today. It's about a trust fund I set up for Trinny shortly after she was born. It's due to mature next month. She would have received two hundred thousand pounds."

"Oh, I see," said Ashley, not knowing why Roger was telling her.

"I've made a decision. I know it's your birthday soon. Remind me. How old will you be?"

"I'll be twenty-one."

"Oh, to be that age again. The month after your birthday, I'll be hitting forty-seven. Where does the time go?"

"Anyway, as I was about to say. The money that would have gone to Trinny ... I'm going to give it to you. I want you to use it to buy a house."

Ashley looked up as she laid out the food. She thought for a moment.

"That's very generous, Roger. Are you saying you want me to move out?"

Roger blinked, and his eyes widened as he realised what he'd said.

"What, oh goodness no. Sorry, I should have explained myself better. I want you to buy a house for the future. I never want you to leave here, but one day, you'll find someone and want to share your life with them and start a family. It's just that property is the best investment. Prices are going up, and it's a good proposition. But I'm giving you the money with no strings. What you do with it is entirely up to you. It was just a suggestion. But the choice is yours. The same way it would have been Trinny's if she was still here."

"Thank you, Roger. That's incredibly generous of you. I appreciate everything you've done for me. I don't know what to say."

"You really don't have to say anything. It's me who should be thanking you. I don't think I could have coped on my own. You brought Trinny back from the brink, and thanks to you, I had an extra couple of very happy years with my daughter. And since then, you've been everything. The closest thing to family I could ever wish for. You're a lovely person, Ashley. I'm so glad you came into my life. And I know Trinny thought the same."

Ashley got up from her chair and hugged Roger.

"Thank you, Roger. Thank you from the bottom of my heart."

TWENTY-FOUR

2008

"Five! Four! Three! Two! One! Happy New Year!"

The party to welcome in 2008 was at its climax. Roger and Ashley were enjoying the celebrations, and all thoughts of the tragedies from the past few years had gone from their minds. At least for tonight.

Back at work, despite Ashley's apprehension, Roger had decided to put everything he had into his most ambitious project yet.

Six months earlier, one of the largest house builders in the area had decided to pull out of a four-acre building project to build a new estate on the edge of Cherrywood. It was the largest plot of land to come to the market in fifteen years. It had planning permission for forty-two luxury houses. Roger had decided to take it over.

The project was massive. Far larger than anything Roger had attempted before. He and Ashley had discussed bringing in outside help, but as the weeks passed, the companies who initially seemed keen to get involved were one by one saying they were no longer interested.

The country had entered a recession, and each week was seeing a dip in the value of houses. A large number of property developers were going bust.

Roger had borrowed two million pounds from the bank and put in two million of his own money. At the time, the projected return was seven and a half million, giving him a comfortable profit.

The loan repayments would kick in soon. So, with all the companies deciding not to become involved, Roger thought it would be wise to sell some of the land and recoup at least a million.

With no property developers prepared to invest, Ashley came up with an idea. Selling some of the plots to people interested in self-build houses. They would probably lose money, but with each passing week, the situation was getting worse. The banks are not known for their patience and would not wait for their money. In the end, Roger made the decision to sell everything he had. That included his house and his shares portfolio. With the money he raised, he could pay off the bank.

2009

Roger had finally managed to pay off the loan. He'd had to sell his house for a knock-down price. He and Ashley had moved into the three-bedroomed house she had purchased when Roger had given her the money from Trinny's trust fund. She'd been renting it out since then.

So they were finally solvent, with the bank loan repaid, although money was tight. Roger had been forced to close his property company. The situation had taken a toll on his health. He was fifty, but nowadays, he looked more like a man of seventy. Ashley decided it was her turn to look after him, as he'd done for her.

"Roger, I've found a job. It's not much, but it will be enough for us to live on."

"I should start looking, too. I'll start phoning around and see if I can find a job as well. With all of my contacts, I should be able to find someone who could use my expertise."

"There's no need for that," said Ashley. "With what I'll be bringing in, if we are careful, we can manage."

"It's not fair to put all the burden on you, Ashley."

"Roger, you took me in when I really needed it. Now it's my turn to repay you. I'm happy to do it. Honestly."

The job Ashley had taken was as a wedding and events coordinator. It hadn't been her first choice, but now that she'd been working for the Gulliver's Events Company for a week, she was surprised how much she was enjoying it.

Each day was a fresh challenge, but that was something she thrived on. It soon became clear she was the most organised person in the office. The other members of staff all had their areas of expertise. But they often failed to spot potential problems before they arose or left out small details. Ashley usually noticed and would quietly take care of them without telling anyone. She was making other people look good without bringing what she had done to anyone's attention.

Each month, she was learning more about the ins and outs of the business. She was offering to take on more and more responsibility. This suited a couple of people who spent most of their time on Facebook or Myspace.

The company was owned by a corporation based in Birmingham. This was one of four branches that organised weddings and other types of events. There was an area manager who would visit once every two weeks. But he didn't seem interested in anything more than the financial targets. As far as Ashley could see, the directors of the business had never visited. It seemed only the branch manager got to speak to them. But as the only other job she'd ever had was working for Roger, she didn't know if this was normal.

After working for the company for six months, Ashley was told that, according to the office rota, she was due to take a week's paid holiday. This was company policy, so no two people were away at the same time.

Although Roger's company had no income, it still owned three small plots of land and a commercial property in the town centre. The three plots all had planning permission for development. Roger had received an offer for one of them. It had originally been worth £800,000, but thanks to the recession, in the current market, the best offer he had was £360,000. Roger accepted it, and with part of the money, he purchased a ten-month-old BMW with only 6,400 miles on the clock.

He asked Ashley if she would like to go away for a few days' holiday, and she readily agreed. They drove up to Blackpool to see the turning-on of the illuminations. And it was nice to get away and enjoy just walking and having someone else prepare all the meals.

They walked along the promenade, visited the tower and watched a couple of shows. One of them was a small club with three drag acts on the bill. A night they thoroughly enjoyed.

But all too soon, the week was over, and they returned home. Roger looked a little better, but she was still worried about him.

As Ashley walked into work on Monday morning, she could tell there was a problem. While she had been away, a number of things had not been taken care of, with the result that a large wedding reception had been double-booked. The bride's father was a friend of the owners, and one of the company directors was currently in the manager's office.

Suddenly, the office door, which had been firmly shut, opened, and the manager walked out.

"Jennifer, could you go into the conference room, please? And take your appointments file with you. We'll meet you there in a short while."

Ashley knew it was serious; the conference room was hardly ever used.

Jennifer was one of the people who spent most of their time on social media. Ashley had often had to remind her of things she'd forgotten to do, or she would undertake whatever needed to be done on Jennifer's behalf.

The entire office staff watched as the manager and the director walked into the conference room.

Fifteen minutes later, the door opened.

"Ashley, could you come in and bring your appointments file with you, please?"

She walked in and was presented to a lady who was introduced as one of the company directors.

"Please sit down," said the manager.

"Last week, while you were away on holiday, we had the

wedding of Mr and Mrs Nelson. However, there was a major problem because the hotel venue had been double-booked."

"Jennifer has told us you didn't make her aware that the venue had a previous booking. She said you were supposed to send her several files and emails, but she never received them."

"That's very strange," replied Ashley. "I sent her all of the files and, over the past month, a bunch of emails updating her on the situation."

"But I never received anything," said Jennifer. "I've checked my computer, but there's nothing there. I wonder if Ashley has copies on her computer."

Ashley sat back in her chair. The smirk on Jennifer's face was now a shallow smile. She looked over with her head slightly to one side. As if she was saying to Ashley, Got you.

The manager spoke.

"Jennifer is right, Ashley. I checked your files, and there is nothing there. No emails or correspondence."

Ashley pointed to the manager's laptop.

"Can I borrow your computer for a minute, please?"

The manager passed it across.

She saw the smile disappear from Jennifer's face, replaced by a puzzled look.

Ashley took a memory stick out of her pocket and plugged it into the slot on the side of the manager's laptop. From there, she was able to restore the zip file backup she had created. It included all of the emails for the past month.

"There we are," said Ashley. She turned the laptop so the manager and director could see the screen with a folder showing all the emails she had backed up.

The room was so quiet you could hear a pin drop.

The two women spent the next two minutes reading the messages.

Ashley looked over at Jennifer and smiled.

As the two women looked up, Ashley continued.

"As you can see, the files I've shown you are backups.

"I noticed someone had accessed my workstation before I arrived for work. You might want to check the CCTV and see who came to the office just after six this morning. Whoever it was logged on to my workstation and deleted the emails from my computer. "And to prove what I have shown you is correct," said Ashley, "here is my appointments file. It lists everything in detail. I locked it in my desk drawer when I went on holiday. And as you can see, it has copies of the memos listing everything that needed to be done that I sent before I went away last week. There are details of what I gave out, and the last sheet is where each person signed to say they had received the documents, as per company policy. It includes Jennifer's signature that she received them."

The director looked up over her glasses at Ashley and then at Jennifer.

"So, Jennifer. What have you got to say for yourself?"

"It's all lies. She's made it all up."

The director looked up. "I don't think it's possible to make this up. It's all here and documented."

The director looked at Ashley. "Do you think we don't monitor things? We have been aware for some time now that you cover for other people when they might fail to complete a project. I am satisfied that you did give Jennifer the list and that she failed to complete the work. Thank you, Ashley. You may go now."

Ashley got up and left the room, and returned to her desk. She decided the best thing to do was to get on with her work. What happened next was not down to her. She did notice the manager going over to Jennifer's desk and then walking back to the conference room.

Five minutes later, Jennifer came rushing out of the conference room. Her face was red, and it was apparent she'd been crying.

"This is all your fault," she screamed at Ashley. And then she stormed out of the office.

The director, followed by the manager, came to the centre of the open-plan office.

"Could I have everyone's attention, please?" said the director.

"Due to the poor work ethic of one of your colleagues, we had a disaster with a wedding over the weekend. Having seen the paperwork, I can assure you the only," – and she emphasised the word only – "person who was responsible has now left the company.

"I would remind you that the work we do is important. There is a bride whose wedding day has been ruined. This is not acceptable. I know one of your colleagues has been covering for one or two people who don't seem to take their responsibilities seriously enough. If that is the case, I would suggest those people consider finding alternative employment. Starting today. I will be monitoring things a little more closely. Thank you for your time."

And with that, she left. No goodbyes, not even to the manager.

Once the manager returned to her office and closed the door, two of the team came over to Ashley.

"We heard what Jennifer said. She was a lazy cow. Don't let what she said get to you."

Ashley said thank you and assured them it wouldn't.

After Ashley had returned from lunch and just sat down at her desk, the manager came out of her office.

"Hi, Ashley. Could you pop into my office?"

She followed the manager.

"Shut the door, please, and sit down.

"I've been reviewing your appointments file and the work you've been doing since you joined. I have to say, I underestimated you. You've been doing a bit more than I realised. You've been making sure one or two other team members got the credit for your work. If you weren't on holiday, then the disaster we had over the weekend wouldn't have happened. I would like to offer you a role with more responsibility. One where you can stretch those undoubted organisational talents you have. It would mean getting out in the field and meeting with some clients. You would be visiting wedding venues and liaising with suppliers directly. Does that sound of interest?" "Yes, it certainly does. And would I see a salary increase to go with it?"

The manager laughed. "You like plain talking, don't you? Yes, we were thinking of an extra three thousand per annum. How does that sound?"

"That sounds fine by me."

"Good. Let's find you your first assignment, then. We have a big wedding just booked in. Two hundred guests, but I'm sure you'll find it a walk in the park."

Ashley smiled. *Only two hundred,* she thought. *I can handle that.*

TWENTY-FIVE

2010

Ashley's manager called her into the office. "Would you be willing to change your holiday from July to August?"

"Well, it is six months away, so that's fine. Is there a reason why?"

"We have a client who isn't happy with her current wedding organiser. The church and reception venues are booked, but that's about it. She's saying we were recommended after a wedding you organised last year.

"It's not a massive wedding. Around eighty guests, but the budget is top-end. From what I hear, she's an absolute nightmare of a client, but the budget is half a million. She wants the best of everything. Apparently, she was a bit of a minor celebrity ten years ago. I think it was on a TV reality show, something like Big Brother or one of those, and now she runs an online dating agency called MyFriendWantsA-Date.com.

"I'm told she's making an absolute fortune from it. It

works by allowing your friends to fill in your profile and deciding which photos of you to upload."

Over the next six months, Ashley spent as much time working on the wedding for this one client as she did for all of the other weddings combined.

Thankfully, everything on the day went like clockwork. Any tiny hitches that always occur were sorted out long before they became a problem. The bride looked radiant, and the weather was perfect. The reception was a huge success. Ashley stayed in the background, ready to cover for anything that might happen, but she needn't have worried.

Just before the bride left for her honeymoon, she came over to Ashley.

"I just wanted to thank you. The day has been stunning. I couldn't have asked for more. You certainly know how to organise things. Here's my card. Call me in two weeks. I might have a job for you, and I'll pay you far more than your current salary."

Ashley thanked her and took the business card. She thought no more about it.

Three weeks later, it was lunchtime, and Ashley was sitting at her desk. She had just returned from the deli with a tuna sandwich and a bottle of water.

Her phone rang.

"Hello. Ashley McDonald."

"Hello, It's Ivy. Mrs Ivy Upton since my wedding."

"Oh, hello, Ivy. How was the honeymoon?"

"It was wonderful. But I wanted to chat with you about something. Is now a good time?"

"Yes, it's fine. I'm just sitting here eating a spot of lunch."

"I won't keep you long. I just wondered if you had thought any more about what I said. You know, with regards to you coming to work for me?"

"To be honest, I thought it was because you had enjoyed the day. I didn't think you were serious."

"I was deadly serious. I saw how much you put into the planning. I noticed how well you took care of everything, and I need someone like you to be involved in my business. You know I run an online dating agency, don't you?"

"Yes. It was part of my research into you so I could understand what you might like. I figured you chose the colours you use on your website and the style of things. It gave me a starting point for the theme for your wedding."

"I see. That's very clever. And it just shows how detailed you are, and that's exactly what I need. Someone with flair and imagination as well as the ability to organise every tiny detail. Why don't you send me your CV, and then we can arrange a meeting."

"I don't have a CV. Outside of working for my father's company, this is the only job I've ever had."

"Okay. Well, what about your education? Which university did you attend?"

"I'm sorry. I haven't been to university."

"But you seem educated and knowledgeable about business."

"I taught myself. I did Open University courses in my spare time."

"Are you being serious?"

"Yes, I am."

"That's amazing. I'm even more impressed."

"I would certainly be interested in the job, but the only problem I can see is that you're based in Manchester."

"It's only an hour on the train. I checked. Why don't you come and visit us for a day and see what we do? Then, if you like what you see, we can discuss things further. What do you say? We don't bite!"

Ashley laughed.

She arranged to visit on Thursday, which was her next day off.

As Ashley had been told, the train took just under an hour to reach Manchester Piccadilly station. The offices for My Friend Wants a Date were situated on Travis Street, which was a pleasant three-minute walk.

Ivy greeted her after she had been buzzed through the security door between reception and the offices. "So glad you could make it. Let's go to my office, and then I'll give you the tour, such as it is."

Ivy made them both a coffee with the Nespresso coffee machine hidden behind a sliding door at the rear of her desk. Then they sat down on the Italian leather chairs in the bay window area of Ivy's impressive office.

After Ivy had given Ashley a tour of the business, they walked back to her office.

"So there we are. What do you think? Is this somewhere you could see yourself working?"

"It's a lovely office, and from what you've described, it's certainly a fresh challenge."

"Does it help that I'm prepared to pay you twice your current salary?"

Ashley laughed. "It certainly helps, but if I didn't think I'd enjoy it or could do it, then it wouldn't matter."

"How much notice do you have to give?"

"Normally, it would be four weeks. However, some big events are coming up, and I wouldn't feel happy leaving them in the lurch, so I'd like to say two months. But I can let you know if they want me to leave sooner."

"You're very loyal. I admire that."

Ivy walked with Ashley to the reception area. The two women shook hands.

"I'll send your employment agreement through in the next few days and then wait to hear from you for a start date."

Ashley walked down the single flight of stairs and onto the street. The sun was shining. Maybe she would check out some local places for lunch so she had her bearings of the area when she started work.

TWENTY-SIX

2011

Good as her word, Ashley stayed on for two months before leaving the events company for the final time. Now, she was sitting on the train to Manchester. She was looking forward to starting her new career at MyFriendWantsADate.com.

She had arrived twenty-five minutes early, so she decided to pop into the deli she had seen on her previous visit. She grabbed some items for her lunch, plus a couple of bars of chocolate, just in case she got the munchies.

She walked into the office with ten minutes to spare.

First thing every Monday morning, the office of MyFriendWantsADate.com all sat down together.

The thirty-minute meeting was split into four sections:

What clients are saying about the service they are receiving.

Are members of staff happy with everything? Are there any problems or situations that need to be addressed? (Staff could also send Ivy a private message if they wanted to discuss something one-to-one.)

Is there anything that can be done better or in a different way to improve the service or the running of the business?

A chance to discuss anything else.

With the agreement of the staff members, each session was recorded onto a Dictaphone. This was so it could be transcribed, and copies were later handed out to everyone who attended.

It was an excellent way for Ashley to meet the other staff members and see how the business was run. She wished they'd had something like it at the wedding events company.

She thought many problems could have been solved or avoided altogether.

As the weeks passed, Ashley loved going to work every day. By and large, the people were a fantastic team, and Ivy was, in her opinion, the best boss she could possibly have. She was a powerhouse and inspired everyone to be the best they could possibly be.

She was learning so much from her. The pair often sat down together to discuss work issues. Ivy would tell Ashley all the details about how she had built up the business from nothing.

2013

For the next two years, everything was perfect. Then things started to change.

At the end of the month, the salaries had failed to be

paid. She had blamed the payroll company, but the staff had noticed other things that were not like Ivy.

And the following Monday, Ivy missed the weekly meeting. She had started to snap at people over little things, such as items of washing up being left in the kitchen overnight.

On Thursday, she shouted at one of the team for arriving ten minutes late. Ashley decided it was time to find out what was wrong. She knocked and marched into Ivy's office. "Ivy. Something is very wrong."

Ivy had been studying something on her desk. She looked up.

"What's the problem?"

"The way you've been acting recently. It's not you. No one has said anything, but I'm sure, like me, they are worried about you."

"It's nothing."

"I'm sorry but that's not good enough."

"How dare you talk to me like that. Remember, I'm your boss."

"Yes, you are. And until now, you've been the best boss anyone could ever wish for. One of the nicest people it's been my privilege to know. But something has changed. And I want to know what it is, so maybe I can help. We can all help. Is the business in financial trouble?"

Ivy laughed. "Good God, no. Nothing like that. You can see how well things are going. No, it's personal."

Ashley could read between the lines.

"You're ill, aren't you? Or your husband. I saw it with my mum before she died. I can see it again now."

"I guess you'll find out soon enough. Everyone will. I've got cancer. It's terminal. They say I might only have a couple of months."

"Oh, Ivy, I'm so sorry. I know words are no consolation. Look. The team can cope with everything. And miracles do happen. Maybe some treatment overseas?"

"I've spent the past month searching and seen four specialists. They all say it's gone too far. I have to accept my fate. Jack and I were planning to have kids. That's what makes me sad. If I could have left him a son or daughter, but..." She shook her head, pushed her chair back from her desk and looked toward her office door. "I guess now would be as good a time as any to tell everyone. Can you gather them all together for me, Ashley?"

"Yes, of course I can, Ivy. But before I do, can I just tell you it is an absolute privilege to work with you. I regard myself as being so lucky. My early years were not great, and then I met Roger. He's not my real father. He took me in when I was at rock bottom and treated me as his own. And then I met you. So, from the bottom of my heart, please know I will be eternally grateful for your belief in me, your support and our friendship. It means the world to me. You mean the world to me."

"Thank you, Ashley. I think you had better go now and find everyone before I burst into tears."

Ashley went off to get everyone together. As she did, the tears started to run down her face. She was thinking that everyone was worried the company was going bust. It would have been better if that were the case.

She had everyone assembled in the main office.

"Ivy has an announcement to make. Let me go and get her."

Ashley walked into her boss's office.

"Everyone's ready, Ivy. I'm sure they will all—" Ashley

stopped in her tracks and looked at Ivy slumped in her office chair.

The doctors had been wrong. She hadn't had two months left. She'd had only two minutes.

The entire team were in deep shock. Ashley suggested that everyone go home for the day and return the following morning to discuss what would happen next.

The next day, most of the staff members arrived early. Three people failed to turn up. The ones who did were anxious to know what was going to happen. It gave some of them the creeps to think Ivy had died so suddenly and in the office.

Ashley stood up. "First of all, I think it would be nice if we had a minute's silence for Ivy to show our respect."

Everyone bowed their heads for sixty seconds.

Ashley continued. "We don't know what Ivy's husband is going to do. So, for now, I feel we need to carry on as best we can. I'm sure he will be in touch, but personally, I don't feel like contacting him at this point. I'm sure he has other things on his mind. And besides, we owe it to the clients of the company. For them, life goes on."

Every day was always busy, with the phones starting to ring from nine o'clock, and today was no exception.

At a few minutes past noon, a man in an expensive suit, with an official look to him, walked into the office.

He placed his briefcase down by his side. Then, in a loud voice, he said, "Excuse me, everyone, could I have your attention, please? Those of you on the phone, please finish your business and then if you would gather round. I'm the company solicitor, Stephen Franks."

Once all the calls had been finished, the team members gathered around where he stood.

"Thank you all. I'm obviously here after the sad loss of Ivy Upton.

"It appears, although she hoped to discuss her situation with you all, things moved faster than anyone could anticipate. She had spoken to her husband about what would happen. As you can imagine, he is in shock right now, so he has asked me to come down here and assure you all that the business will continue. Everyone will get paid as usual, and he asks if you can continue running the company until he feels able to take things over.

"I will leave my details, and if any of you have any problems, I would ask you to contact me, and I will sort them out.

"The funeral date hasn't been arranged yet, but you will be told when it is, and if you wish to attend, you will be most welcome. The office will be closed on the day as a mark of respect. Do any of you have any questions?"

Everyone remained silent.

Mr Franks passed out a sheet of paper with his contact details, then picked up his briefcase and left.

An hour later, as Ashley was sitting at her desk eating the lunch she had brought in, two girls came over.

"Hey, Ashley. We just wondered what you are planning to do. Will you stay, or will you look for something else now?"

"For the moment, I have no plans to leave. I think that would be a problem for the company, and I wouldn't want to do anything that would cause a complication. Why do you ask?"

"Now that Ivy isn't here, we're worried about what will happen. Who do you think will take over from her?"

"It's not something I've given a lot of thought to. Ivy only passed away yesterday. All I want to do is make sure the business continues. It's the least we can do."

Ashley wasn't surprised. There hadn't been much work done in the office this morning. Everyone was gathering in small groups and whispering. She thought that was disrespectful, but there was nothing she could do about it. She assumed that Ivy's husband would run the business or that her family would bring in someone as manager. Ivy had usually been in the office two days a week. The business was well organised, so it could run for quite some time without anyone. But right now, all she could do was think about Ivy. A beautiful person with everything to live for. Yet now she was gone. Life can be so cruel.

TWENTY-SEVEN

2013

Three days later, there was a message from Mr Franks, letting everyone know when Ivy's funeral would be and where it would be held. As the solicitor had said, the entire office would be closed for the day. People could either attend or take the day off; it was their decision. Ashley knew she would attend the funeral out of respect and informed the solicitor.

The funeral started at 11 a.m., and Ashley was introduced to Ivy's parents. It was probably the saddest day of their lives, especially as Ivy was their only child. It was a sad day for everyone.

Ivy's father walked over to Ashley at the reception. "Thank you for coming. We both appreciate what you are doing by keeping the business running. We can understand that you may be wondering what will happen. It's been hard to think of anything but the arrangements over the past few days. We'll make an announcement in the next week as to what happens next, but what I can say is that the business will continue."

"Thank you. I'll let everyone know. I know some of the staff aren't here today. It's just that they want to remember Ivy as she was. They were too upset to attend. It's not that they don't care."

"No, I fully understand. These things affect people in different ways."

Ashley was one of the last people to leave and said her final goodbyes to Ivy's parents and husband. He stood in the corner of the room with his head down, looking shell-shocked. Ashley had briefly spoken to him, but she didn't think he'd heard a word she said.

When she finally got home, Roger had already started to prepare the evening meal.

"How did it go?" he asked.

"Let's put it this way – it's not a situation I would like to repeat. I still can't believe she's gone."

"Ashley, I've been thinking long and hard. I guess the situation with your boss has brought it to the front of my mind."

"Is something wrong?"

"No. No. What I'm trying to say, in my own clumsy way, is one day, I'll be gone, and you'll be alone. We have to face facts. So I want to set things up so you are provided for. If the law allowed, I would ask if you wanted to become my adopted daughter, but that stops when a person becomes eighteen. I'm going to see my solicitor tomorrow and make sure you are in my will."

"You make it sound like you're ninety. You're still young.

You might find someone else and get married again. So don't be hasty."

"I tried marriage once. Look how that turned out. So, no thanks. The only person in my life nowadays is you."

Ashley could feel the tears well in her eyes.

She walked over and gave him a big hug.

TWENTY-EIGHT

2013

It had been three weeks since the funeral. The company solicitor made a brief appearance every Friday, but otherwise, they hadn't heard anything from the family.

However, on his next visit, Mr Franks looked more serious than usual. Ashley knew something was coming. They all did.

"I have an announcement to make. I am here to let you know that, after due consideration from the family, it has been decided to sell the business to a new owner. Everything will continue as normal, and you have my assurance there will be no job losses. The new owners are keen to keep everything as it is. The agreement has been signed, and the new owners take over from next month.

"A representative, a gentleman by the name of Charles Whitehead, will be coming here next Wednesday, which is the first of the month.

"I also have to tell you that Ivy left each of you something in her will. For every year you have worked here, you will receive a tax-free gift of one thousand pounds. If you have worked here less than a year, you will receive five hundred pounds. Are there any questions?"

Four people called out the same question at the same time.

"Who are the new owners?"

"They are one of the top US online dating agencies, Cupid's Arrow."

"Oh no," said Victoria. "I used to work for them when I lived in New York. They took over a small dating agency I worked for, and they are not a good company. I quit after two months, and so did a lot of other people. I thought I recognised his name, Charles Whitehead. We used to call him Mr Knucklehead because that's what he is. He's just a bean counter. He doesn't care about people, just the money."

"Now, now," said Mr Franks. "I'm sure everything will be fine. They've given assurances that all your jobs will be retained."

"Yes," piped up Victoria, "but they make life unbearable until half the people leave. That's what they do. You mark my words – this place will be unrecognisable in a few weeks. Welcome to hell!"

TWENTY-NINE

2013

The following week, when Charles Whitehead arrived, he gathered everyone together. He told them exactly the same as the solicitor had said: jobs would be safe, and everything would carry on as before – they would hardly notice the difference.

He said the only thing to change would be the name of the company. It would change from My Friend Wants a Date, to Cupid's Arrow Dating.

Charles took over Ivy's office. The solicitor had already sent someone to clear out Ivy's possessions, and a cleaning contractor had come in to ensure it was clean and tidy. There was a new sign on Ivy's office door:

Charles Whitehead
Vice President

Business continued at the same pace as before, and with

the staff levels they had, they could just about cope. However, Victoria, good as her word, had given in her notice, and it was now her final week. Two other girls who were friends with her had done the same.

Everyone was wondering when the new staff members would arrive.

Charles called a staff meeting.

"Our analysts have been looking at the figures for the business and the running costs. Our promise was that all of your jobs would be secure, and that's still the case. However, we cannot afford to replace the three members of staff who will leave us at the end of this week. So, I've prepared a new rota for each of you to take over some of their responsibilities. I know I can count on you all to work together. Thank you for your time."

And with that, he was gone, back to the office that had once been Ivy's.

The following week, another person gave notice, and it didn't look like they were going to be replaced when they left. So, with each passing week, the workload grew.

Ashley was getting home later and later and more exhausted.

One evening at seven o'clock, she was still in the office when the phone rang. It was a voice she recognised.

"I have an idea," said Roger. "Why don't you start your own online dating agency? You can see there are people making a lot of money from it. Ivy must have started from zero. Didn't you say she had told you all about how she got the business established?"

"I couldn't do that. I don't have enough money for a start."

"Well, I didn't tell you, but I managed to sell some of the

land from the Cherrywood plot. With what I had from the other parcels I've sold; I have a spare half a million. That should be enough, don't you think?"

"No. That's money you might need for later in life."

"Don't worry about me. I've been investing into a private pension since I was twenty-five. When I turn sixty, I'm going to be sitting pretty."

"It's a nice idea, Roger, and I appreciate it, I really do, but I don't think so."

"I tell you what. Give it some thought. Think over the type of clients you would go after. Would you copy Ivy or perhaps go after another sector. You were on at me to start dating. I didn't mention it, but I had a look online. There's not a lot out there for people of my age group. I spoke to three ladies this afternoon, and they were saying the same."

"Where was that?"

"At the library."

"My, my. You're a dark horse. Talking to ladies about dating websites. Besides, I thought you didn't like going to the library in town."

"I don't. The Fenton Road branch has reopened. Totally rebuilt. They've kept the original entrance doors. And it's lovely inside. For once, the council have got something right."

"Find any good books?"

"Yes. I found what looks like a really good one by Josephine Tey."

She heard him laugh. "What's so funny?"

"I was speaking to the ladies as I was standing in a queue to take out a book called The Man in the Queue."

Ashley laughed. "Anyway," she continued. "Regarding your idea, I'll think about it, but I'm not promising."

"That's all I ask. Please give it some thought. Maybe one

for ladies in their later years. I checked online for the domain name LaterYears.com, but that's been taken. However, I found LaterLadies.com, and that's available. What do you think of the name?"

Ashley smiled. "I appreciate the offer. Let me think about it."

"Don't think for too long; otherwise, the name could be taken."

As she sat on the train on her journey home, Ashley started to seriously consider the idea Roger had proposed earlier.

What annoyed everyone was that Ivy had always been very open about the business's finances. They knew the company made a profit but weren't sure how much. The staff had discussed it and thought maybe it made around a hundred thousand pounds profit a year.

When she got home, she discussed it with Roger.

"Why don't you go on to the Companies House website? You can download copies of the company accounts, and you'll be able to figure out how much they make."

Ten minutes later, the inkjet printer on Roger's desk was printing out a copy of the accounts of My Friend Wants a Date Limited.

Ashley picked up the printed sheets and laid them across the dining room table. From the bookkeeping course she'd taken a few years ago, she understood what it all meant.

She turned to Roger. "There we are ... look at that. Turnover for the year before last was just under two million, with profits of ... I don't believe it ... eight hundred thousand pounds. Last year the turnover increased to over three million. And the profit was one point six million. And they are telling us they can't afford to employ more people."

The following morning, Ashley took the financial accounting information into the office. She showed the printed sheets from Companies House to the other girls in the team. "I think it's disgusting. They're making all that money, and they don't want to replace anyone," said Zara, who was about to go on maternity leave.

She went on. "It just shows how greedy they are. Ivy built this place up from nothing. I remember when I first started working here. She was here when I arrived each morning at eight o'clock, and she was still working away when I left at five. And I know she came in over the week-ends. It's bloody disgusting what they are doing if you ask me."

When Charles arrived, everyone returned to their desk and got on with their work. No one said anything to him.

At the end of the day, just as she was leaving, Ashley decided to speak with Charles.

She knocked on his office door.

"Come in."

"Hello, Charles. I just wondered, when Zara goes on maternity leave in two weeks, will there be someone to replace her?"

"I'm not sure at the moment. A final decision hasn't been made yet. We have to consider our shareholders, and the budget is tight. But we'll do what we can."

"Okay, thank you. I just wondered."

It was looking more and more like what Victoria had told them before she left had been right. The way things were going, the UK part of the business would become the same as she had experienced when she worked for them in New York.

The company's shareholders got the lion's share of the

profits, and if there were any scraps left over, they were given to the staff.

Ashley picked up her phone and called Roger.

"I'll be home at eight-thirty. I think I'm ready to discuss your idea."

"In that case, I'll put the food on ready for when you get in."

"Don't go to any trouble. I'm only thinking about it. I haven't made up my mind yet."

THIRTY

2013

It was just after eight-thirty when Ashley arrived home. She called out, "I'm home."

"I'm in the kitchen," came the reply.

She walked through to see the table all set for the meal. In the middle was a silver bucket with what looked like an expensive bottle of champagne.

"Are we celebrating something?"

"Yes. You starting your new business."

"I told you I was still thinking about it."

"Yes. But you have, and you've decided to give it a go, haven't you?"

"How on earth did you know?"

Roger laughed. "Men have intuition too, you know. Not often, but occasionally. I'm right, aren't I?"

Ashley gave him a big smile. "Yes, on this rare occasion, you're right."

He smiled, punching the air. "Yes. Knew it!"

Roger served up their meal and opened the champagne. He pulled out the cork. It didn't disappoint and gave a loud pop!

"Here's to your online dating agency," said Roger.

"I'll drink to that."

"Have you thought of a name yet?"

"I'll use the one you came up with."

"You like the name then?"

"It's grown on me, and I haven't been able to think of a better one. So here's to LaterLadies. Cheers!"

"Cheers!" echoed Roger.

Over the following four months, the pair spent all their spare time researching the market into online dating agencies. They knew it wouldn't be easy. A lot of people had tried and failed in the past. However, all their research told them this market sector was underserved, and demand was increasing.

The domain names had been purchased. A graphic designer had been engaged to give the brand an upmarket image. Roger had even found a small suite of offices, although they hadn't yet signed the lease. The software had been purchased and set up, and the website and the interface that greeted potential clients was now in place. Everything was on track, and things were coming together.

The time was fast approaching when Ashley would hand in her notice to quit working for the new owners of Ivy's business.

One afternoon, Ashley returned from lunch and saw two men in the office with Charles.

"Who are they?" she asked one of the girls sitting in the office eating lunch.

"They are from a company called OFD. It's short for

'Old Fish Dating'. They run a small dating agency for older ladies, and Charles says the company might be buying their business."

Ashley and Roger had looked at the company during their research. As far as they could make out, they had about eight hundred clients, which was extremely small compared to how many were on the books of Cupid's Arrow Dating.

But Ashley had an idea: they had eight hundred more than LaterLadies. Making a bid for their company would make good financial sense if the price was right.

That way, they could hit the ground running and build it with a good list of clients rather than start from nothing.

During a mid-afternoon break, Ashley went for a walk and phoned Roger.

"Where are you?"

"I'm in Fenton Road Library. I'm just taking back a couple of books. I'm in the queue to return the book The Man in the Queue."

Ashley laughed. "You've used that before when you took the book out."

"In that case, I guess I'd better return the other book as well."

"Which one is that?"

"How to Become a Comedian."

She laughed again. "Yes, a complete waste of time for you."

"Cheeky."

"I've got something that might interest you more."

Ashley told him about the meeting between Charles and the two men.

"Now that sounds promising. If you can email me the details of this company, I'll get straight on to it, make an approach and see if they are open to other offers. I think you're right. It makes perfect sense to have a database of clients in place when we start."

So far, they hadn't registered a limited company. Roger had suggested they wait until the last possible moment so no one knew what they were planning. Once you register with Companies House it becomes public knowledge. Then you start getting contacted by all sorts of companies and people who know what you are planning. He decided it was far better for them to have a surprise on their side.

THIRTY-ONE

When Ashley arrived home, Roger stood by the front door with a big grin.

"You look pleased with yourself."

"Yes. I've got a meeting with the two directors of Old Fish Dating. I got the impression they weren't over the moon with the offer from your boss. If we can come up with a fair deal, I think they'll be inclined to take it. It seems he might have rubbed them up the wrong way. It didn't sound like they took to him.

"They even told me they overheard one of the staff call him Mr Knucklehead instead of Mr Whitehead. They said they agreed."

"Wow. It would be great if we could start with eight hundred clients."

"Actually, they now have nine hundred clients."

"Even better."

"I'm seeing them tomorrow. If all goes well, we could have it wrapped up by the end of the week. They already have all the contracts in place, as things were at an advanced stage. I get the impression nothing would delight them more than to tell Mr Knucklehead they've accepted a better offer."

After their meal, the pair sat down at the dining table and started plotting dates and events they could run to make a big splash when they launched. They would offer all the clients from OFD a free trial period. They would run social media and print adverts in publications like The Lady and Yours magazine. Roger said he knew a girl who ran a local public relations company. Perhaps they could obtain her services to help get publicity for the business. The local newspapers and radio stations should be interested in a new local business, especially if they ran a few paid adverts.

Local Parish magazines might be good, and a couple of adverts on local radio.

Ashley had a lot of ideas about how this would be head and shoulders above the other dating agencies. It would be more upmarket. If she had learned one thing from working with Roger, it was that people with money were happy to pay for exclusive services. So, LaterLadies would be more expensive and more upscale than the other agencies out there. And if Ashley had anything to do with it, it would be the best. She looked back at how far she had come in her life. She couldn't have done all of this without Roger. And she had an idea that she hoped would make him happy.

"Sit down, Roger. I have something to ask you.

"Meeting you has been the most wonderful thing in my life. You know my background and what I've been through, and I wouldn't be here without you.

"I know you can't adopt me because I'm over eighteen, but I'd like to do something that tells the world I'm proud to have you as my father. I want to change my surname from McDonald to Springfield. And I'd like to go the whole way. I don't want to be associated with my past before I met you. It still haunts me to think of it. So, instead of Ashley, I'm going to use my middle name, which is Grace. So, with your blessing, I would like to change my name by deed poll to Grace Springfield so everyone knows I'm your daughter. What do you say?"

Ashley saw the tears well up in his eyes.

"Ashley ... er, I mean, Grace ... that would make me the happiest man in the world."

THIRTY-TWO

January 2014

Charles had reduced the number of days he came into the office, and there were constant phone calls from suppliers who hadn't been paid. Office supplies and headed stationery often ran out despite repeated reminders and notes left on his desk.

In fact, everything was extremely lax on the management side. Procedures set in place to ensure clients were receiving the best possible service were being ignored. With the reduced number of staff, it was impossible to cover everything. Ashley was sitting at her desk when the phone rang.

"Good morning. Cupid's Arrow Dating. How may I help?"

"My name is Detective Inspector Carol Meade with Greater Manchester Police. I'd like to speak with someone in charge, please."

Ashley looked across to Charles's office. The light was off. He hadn't arrived yet. "Mr Whitehead, the vice president, is not here at the moment. Perhaps I can assist you. I'm the office manager."

"We're investigating a series of complaints from ladies who say they have been scammed out of large sums of money. Two of these ladies appear to have been members of your dating website."

"Oh dear, that's not very nice. When you say large sums of money, can you say how much we're talking about?"

"One lady reports she's lost twenty-five thousand pounds, and the other lady won't tell us the exact amount, but she says it's well into six figures.

"It appears the ladies were persuaded to lend money to someone they thought could be trusted. It's a scam, of course. These people target more mature women, especially ladies who are lonely and vulnerable. They put up false profiles, pretend to be interested in the women, and tell them they love them. They are extremely good at what they do. We've had doctors, lawyers and even one High Court judge who have been victims. In most cases, they think they are talking to someone who tells them they are working abroad but will be back in the UK soon. They explain that's the reason they cannot meet in person.

"They start by asking for small amounts of money. Telling the ladies things such as they have had an accident and have a hospital bill to pay, and it's a bit more than they thought. Some are extremely clever, and after a couple of weeks, they pay the money back. Then come requests for more significant sums, and it continues until the person either runs out of cash or catches on to what is really happening.

"The fraudsters tend to copy what the woman's profile says they like. So if you say you like certain films or books, they will say they like the same ones. Their goal is to hook you by trying to grab your heart and create a friendship by mirroring what you like. Then, they will try to coax you offline and away from the security of the dating sites.

"It's a booming business. They mainly target women aged forty-five to seventy-five who are looking for a long-term relationship. These women are trusting and receptive to the various sob stories the scammers use and, therefore, are more likely to hand over their cash.

"I presume you do regular checks on such things to protect your clients?"

Ashley knew the answer was no, but she couldn't reveal that to the detective. That was down to Charles and the owners.

As the women chatted, Ashley went on to Google and did a search to see if there had been any problems for the company in the US.

She was amazed when she found an article showing the company was already facing two lawsuits brought in the US by the Federal Trade Commission.

They alleged that clients had been persuaded from the website system to places like WhatsApp or Zoom. And the company had not done enough to prevent it from happening. The result had been that several members had been conned into parting with large sums of money to men they had only met on the dating site.

Now, it looked like the same thing was happening with the UK business and some of their clients are falling for the romance scams.

The detective continued.

"From the information we have, all the online dating websites are coming up against this problem. You are certainly not alone and by no means the one to suffer the most. However, it might be wise for you to put more details about these types of scams on your website to protect your clients. To save your members from being tempted to communicate with men away from the safety of the online system."

Ashley shivered at the thought of what these people were doing.

"I think the best thing for me to do is ask Mr Whitehead to call you when he gets in. Can I take a number where he can reach you?"

The detective gave Ashley the details, and she noted them down. Then, after the call, she copied them and put them on Charles's desk.

As the two women continued to discuss the situation, they were unaware that in a different part of the country, one member of the dating website had already lost a lot of money and, over the next few weeks, would lose considerably more. The lady in question was a high-powered lawyer called Libby Devonshire-Wright.

THIRTY-THREE

April 2014

Maybe her life flashed before her in the brief three seconds it took for Libby Devonshire-Wright to plunge the one hundred and twenty feet from the terrace of her eighth-floor luxury penthouse onto the concrete below. Still, she would never be able to tell anyone.

The wine glass she had been holding had smashed and was lying in pieces all around her.

As Tom Francis cycled toward Cambridge railway station, even at five-thirty on a cold Friday morning, there was a smile on his face. His mate, Paul Cousins, had agreed to swap shifts. Luckily, Paul wasn't a footie fan. That meant Tom could have this coming Saturday off to attend the match. Not just any game. He'd managed to get hold of a ticket to the semi-final.

As Tom turned the corner to Station Road, he noticed someone lying on the ground, close to the new luxury apartments across the plaza from the station.

As he got closer, he could see the outline. It was a woman.

Probably a drunk or one of the druggies who seemed to be creeping into the area at night.

Then he noticed all the red stuff. It was coming from the side of her head.

"Oh, my God. She's dead."

Tom pulled out his phone and dialled 999.

As he waited, he wasn't sure what to do. Should he leave her or go over to the station, where he knew there would be a blanket in the first aid room to cover her?

"I hope they bloody well hurry up and get here," he murmured.

Then, in the distance, he heard the wail of the siren. He knew it wouldn't take them long. At 5.35 a.m., the streets were not exactly busy.

As he saw the police car getting close, he stepped away from the body, lifted his arms and waved in the direction of the vehicle.

Within ten minutes of the first two police officers arriving on the scene, they were joined by two more. Then, the SOCOs came and started to put up a white tent around the body. After a further ten minutes, another vehicle arrived. The two people who got out looked as if they were detectives.

They walked toward the constable holding a clipboard. He was stationed in front of the crime scene tape that had been set up. His job was to prevent anyone unauthorised from gaining access to the cordoned off area.

DI Graham Yates held up his police ID badge for the

constable to see and write down his name on the crime scene log.

The female officer with him did the same, giving her name to the constable. "DS Ella Hudson."

"What have we got, constable?"

"It looks like a lady either fell or jumped from the building. A railway worker on his way to work discovered her lying here."

"Okay. We'll suit up and then have a look."

The two detectives returned to their car; Graham opened the boot and removed overalls, latex gloves, paper shoes and a face mask for each of them. Then they walked back into the tent and spoke with the scenes of crime officer.

There wasn't much they could do. "No signs of ID, I suppose?" asked Ella.

"No, sorry."

"If she fell from this building, we need to see if anyone recognises her. It's lucky she didn't land on her face."

Ella took a close-up photo of the victim's face on her phone, making sure there was no blood in sight. She sent a copy to Graham's mobile.

"You take the even floors, and I'll take the odd," said Graham.

Most people wouldn't appreciate being woken up at six-thirty in the morning, but it had to be done.

Ella had knocked at all the doors on the second and fourth floors with no success. She knocked on the first door on floor six.

After a third time of knocking, Ella was confronted by a girl in her late twenties wearing nothing but a man's white shirt.

Ella held up her police ID at eye level. "Sorry to bother you, but I wonder if you recognise this woman?"

She showed the photo on her phone.

"I-I think my boyfriend works with her. Hang on a sec."

A man, who Ella guessed was in his early thirties, came to the door.

Ella showed him the photo.

"It's not a great photo, but I would say that's Libby. Oh, Libby Devonshire-Wright, she's a partner where I work at Stanhope & Ingham just around the corner."

"Do you know which apartment she lives in?" asked Ella.

"Oh, Libby has the penthouse. Is there something wrong? Silly question, otherwise you wouldn't be here, would you. It's a bit early for my brain, sorry."

"All I can say is there has been a fatality. It looks like someone has fallen from one of the upper-floor apartments."

"Oh, my goodness. That's terrible."

"Yes. We won't be able to confirm anything yet. Do you know if anyone has a key to her penthouse?"

"She has a colleague and friend, Sarah, who lives in the apartment block next door. Fifth floor, apartment five, I think. I recall Libby saying she went in and watered the plants for her recently when she was away for a few days."

Graham and Ella went to Sarah's apartment. After they'd knocked several times, a bleary-eyed woman eventually answered. She looked a little hungover.

They both produced their ID and held it up.

"Hello," said Ella. "We understand you're a friend of Libby Devonshire-Wright?"

"Yes, that's correct. We were together last night. Is there a problem?"

"We need to gain access to her apartment, and we're told you have a key."

"Yes. I do. Is she not answering? Perhaps she's a little hungover. We did have quite a lot to drink."

Ella explained what had happened. Sarah fell sideways against her hallway wall.

"Oh no. Oh no! I shouldn't have left her like that."

Gradually, she seemed to regain some composure.

"I understand it's a shock. But would it be possible for you to come and have a look? See if the apartment is the same as when you left last night."

"Yes, of course. Just a minute. I'll finish getting dressed and fetch the key."

They went to Libby's apartment. Ella knocked at the door of the penthouse. They didn't expect anyone to answer, but you never know.

After knocking three times, Ella used the key from the friend standing behind them in the doorway.

"If you can wait here until we say it's alright. And please don't touch the door or anything."

There was a hallway leading to a large open-plan living and dining area, with the kitchen off to the left at the rear. They could see the terrace area from where they guessed the victim had fallen but didn't go near it until the forensics team had been over it. As they walked back, they saw the doors to the two bedrooms were open. It all looked minimal and tidy. Nothing seemed out of place.

Ella walked out to the hallway. She helped Sarah put on the paper shoes and handed her a pair of latex gloves. Then she walked with her into the apartment so she could check if everything looked much the same as it had done when she was last there.

"It all looks the same. There are the bottles of wine we consumed. I think there were only two when I left. It looks like Libby opened another one. Otherwise, nothing looks any different."

Ella walked with her to her apartment in the next block and thanked her for her assistance. She told Sarah they would need to keep the key to Libby's apartment for now.

Meanwhile, in the tent on the plaza outside the apartments, the doctor had completed all his preliminary tests. He had given permission for Libby's body to be taken away to the mortuary. The forensics team went up to the penthouse to continue their examination. It looked like the victim had either fallen or had been pushed from the large balcony of the apartment. They would search for clues, signs of a struggle or indications that anyone else had been present.

Stanhope & Ingham occupied the top floors of number two Station Road. They specialise in commercial-development law and have a staff of thirty-six people.

Libby Devonshire-Wright, aged fifty-one and a recent divorcee, was a partner of the firm. The walk from her office to the apartment building was less than a hundred yards. The apartment was in the newly completed Station Central apartment complex.

The entire area around Cambridge railway station has recently undergone a significant development. It was now full of trendy café's, mini-supermarkets and sandwich shops.

All sat alongside the high-rise luxury apartments and the impressive glass-fronted office blocks.

The development hadn't been without controversy. The promised health clinic and heritage visitor centre had both failed to materialise. This was thanks to the greedy developers. After agreeing to the facilities, they clawed back as much as possible by watering down and renegotiating their obligations. Each regressive step was argued on the basis of the straitened economic climate in the wake of the recent financial crisis.

The funding had been supplied by Aconda Life and Pensions UK Ltd, and it was built by Crookmead Developments at a total cost of £87 million. Many small businesses and a row of Victorian terraced houses had to be demolished to make way for the development.

The plans were hotly contested by more than seven hundred local residents. There were also objections from the local council. But the plans were approved on appeal to central government over a hundred miles away in London. Approved without a single visit by anyone to check out the details.

Greed was the name of the game. Local council planners with a limited budget were fighting a losing battle against the wealthy developers. When large companies are involved, the latter always wins when it's between amenities and profit.

At the end of the day, money talks.

Graham and Ella arrived at the offices of Stanhope & Ingham at nine-thirty. After showing their ID to the receptionist, they were led into a large conference room.

In the centre was a sizeable maple-colour conference table. The top of the table was exquisitely shiny. The only item on it was the conference call phone in the centre. It was surrounded by eight high-back tan brown leather executive chairs.

The other items in the room were two life-size replica Chinese Terracotta Warrior figures. They stood in the corners. At each end were two five-foot-tall palm trees sitting in pots and a large TV with a DVD player underneath it. One entire wall consisted of six large windows allowing a view of Station Road.

They had been offered a range of drinks but had declined.

Two minutes later, the door opened and in walked a man and lady who the detectives could instantly tell were senior figures in the company.

THIRTY-FOUR

The man and the woman introduced themselves as directors of the firm.

"Good morning. I'm David Hunter."

They both recognised Sarah Cardington, the woman from their tour of Libby's apartment, but looking much more sober.

"Thank you for seeing us." Graham addressed David Hunter. "I'm DI Yates," said Graham, holding up his ID badge, "and this is my partner DS Ella Hudson. I expect Sarah has informed you why we are here."

"Yes. Sarah called me earlier at home with the dreadful news about Libby," said David. "How can we be of help to you?"

"One of the lines of enquiry is that Mrs Devonshire-Wright may have taken her own life. So we are wondering if you can tell us her state of mind and if there might be a reason, she would think of doing such a thing?" asked Graham.

Sarah spoke. "She was a friend as well as a colleague. As

you are aware, I was with her last night. So I think I know what happened. We had a long chat. She confided in me.

"First of all, I have to say that Libby was an intelligent, hard-working woman who, thanks to her outstanding abilities, was at the top of her profession.

"She got divorced about four years ago. Her ex-husband was a doctor. According to what she told me, part of the reason for their divorce was the lack of time they spent together.

"She said it was a shame because, for the first fifteen years of their marriage, things couldn't have been better. Then she began to notice the early signs of the menopause. Of course, there was nothing she could do. It was nature taking its course. She thought their partnership would have been strong enough to withstand it.

"It was only later that she found out he'd had enough time to spend with his secretary at a local hotel. It seemed that over various weekends, he said he was attending lectures. She suspected the lectures were held in hotel bedrooms, with only two attendees. "The way she put it. She said it was just a shame his morals weren't as upstanding as his dick seemed to be with his secretary.

"That was four years ago; recently, she had been ready to move on.

"About three months ago, she told me she had found someone who seemed to care about her and how she felt. Someone who had time for her.

"She had joined an online website called Cupid's Arrow Dating and found three men. Two of them had been local to her, and she had gone on dates with one of the men, but then his job had moved down to London, and the distance had become too much.

"The second man just wasn't right from the start. All he liked was sports; Libby wasn't a great fan of it.

"Then she had come across Colonel Sam Passmore, an American, but he'd lived in England when he was younger and was planning to move back.

"He was on active duty in Afghanistan. It meant there were problems with communications and security. So, instead of using the secure links of the dating agency, they started corresponding via email and WhatsApp. Sam explained that the army was blocking his US Army email account because of his security situation. So he suggested they transfer to his personal account on Yahoo, as it was less strict. Otherwise, it would mean the end of their relationship. That's why many of the messages he told her he'd sent via the dating site hadn't arrived.

"Libby had checked to see if Sam Passmore was genuine, as you can't be too careful on these dating websites. He had insisted that she look into his background. She had found a few things. He explained there wasn't too much because the information had a way of getting into the hands of the Taliban and could put him in danger. "He had sent her copies of correspondence as a way of helping to reassure her. But she really didn't need it. In fact, she told me she hadn't even bothered to check them out.

"She said that she knew simply from talking to him that he was genuine. She said they had so much in common, and he maintained regular contact. He only had four months to go before he retired from the military at fifty-five with, as he put it, a nice fat pension pot.

"He would sell his ranch in North Carolina and move to England, as he had no family or anything to keep him tied to the US.

"With her divorce out of the way, nothing could stop them from getting married.

"And he had already proven himself like the time when the army had mucked up his salary payment. She had lent him three thousand dollars. He paid it back the following month precisely on time, as promised. Despite her insistence, he had paid her interest on the loan. "They had spoken on Skype on a couple of occasions. However, the signal wasn't very good. All Libby could see was a static picture of him that moved occasionally. However, it remained frozen for most of the eight-minute call. At the end, he told her he had blown her a kiss, and the connection had cut out. "She said she loved the sound of his voice. And the poems he had sent her were so romantic and his declarations of undying love.

"Still, it wouldn't be long before they were together, and she could hold him in her arms and give him a real kiss. Four months and counting.

"A month later, they had discussed how he would sell his ranch and then move to England. But there was a problem.

"He told her his ranch was worth two million dollars, but it had fallen into disrepair because he had been away for some time. He needed four hundred thousand dollars to fix it up. He had the money in stocks and shares, but that would take time to organise if he didn't want to lose a lot by selling too quickly. Libby said she would be prepared to loan him the money. He would make it official by getting his lawyer to draw up a loan guarantee.

"Libby was having none of it. Of course, she would lend him the money, and she didn't need some paperwork. She knew how much a lawyer would charge for that. She trusted him. They would be spending the rest of their lives together.

"Due to the security situation in Afghanistan, it was three weeks before they were able to speak on Skype.

"Sam had phoned her to say he had received the money and transferred it to the company carrying out the repairs. Everything was going according to plan, except the builders might need more money, but not for a week or two.

"Just like previous times, Sam could see Libby, but the image of him on her screen was static, just a photo of him. He had explained that she could hear him, but there was no picture due to the US Army's internet security. Still, it didn't matter. They were talking.

"They chatted for a further five minutes. Sam had warned her that the line might suddenly cut out due to the internet security system. And then it did.

"I remember speaking to her six weeks ago. She said it was a matter of weeks before Sam retired. From how she talked, it was like two lovebirds making plans to be together. Sam would need a week in the States to sort out his affairs, and then he would head for England. The sale of his ranch was now underway, and the buyer was anxious to take it over as soon as possible.

"Sam had told Libby to look around and find a nice house in the country where they could be together. She had sent him some photos, but he wanted something grander than the ones she had sent. He would be getting $3.2 million for his ranch, and his pension pot had built up over the years. He would get a nice lump sum and enough for them to spend time together. With the money Libby had, they would be set for life.

"The latest house details Libby had sent were perfect. Sam had fallen in love with the house. Libby wasn't quite as keen, but what did it matter? She wanted to please her man.

At just under two million pounds, it was undoubtedly a large property. However, Sam had told her he made a lot of money from breeding horses on his ranch and planned to do the same in England. So they needed somewhere big.

"Apparently, he had done a private deal with the owners, bypassing the estate agents. He had negotiated a significant discount on the price because he had arranged to pay a percentage in cash. The money would be paid into the seller's overseas bank account. Libby knew this was illegal, but she wouldn't be directly involved. She would go along with it because, at the end of the day, it would save them a great deal of money. "The following week, Sam gave her details of the bank account where he needed her to transfer the money. She was to pay seven hundred thousand to the seller of the house they were buying as a holding deposit. "I was with her last night at her apartment from about six o'clock. We were having a meal together.

"She was expecting a call from Sam at around eight. They had spoken on the phone the previous evening. He was four days away from retirement.

"She said he always called her around that time, so I was getting ready to leave, but last night, there had been no call at eight.

"At just after ten o'clock, her phone rang. She expected to hear a voice she recognised, but it wasn't Sam. The call was from a fellow US Army officer. She listened to what he said, but perhaps she hadn't heard him right. Maybe she got it wrong.

"He informed her that Sam had decided to go out on active duty with his unit for one last time and had been killed by a roadside bomb.

"The officer who rang said he was very sorry to inform

her, but with less than one week left to serve, Sam had been killed in action.

"I stayed with her until about eleven. She said she was going to bed. That she would think about what to do in the morning. I must admit, we'd had a couple of bottles of wine, at least. I somehow stumbled back to my apartment and went to bed. Then the next thing I knew was when you rang my doorbell this morning."

After Sarah had left, Libby wandered over to the drinks cabinet, opened a new bottle of wine, found her glass, filled it and gulped down the contents. When it was empty, she filled it again and did the same. Then, she filled the glass once more. After the bottle was empty, she wandered over to the balcony.

Four thousand, three hundred miles away in Lagos, Nigeria, a young man named Joseph Okechuku sat back in the chair in front of his computer. As he did, a knowing smile spread across his face.

Over the past three months, his bank account had been given a substantial boost thanks to his latest victim. A stupid lady in England who he'd been stringing along.

It was a country he had never visited but planned to in the near future. He was looking forward to his trip. Especially if it was full of women who were as gullible as this one. A woman who had, over the past few months, paid over a million pounds into the bank account of a man who didn't exist.

He loved old buildings and castles. He planned to visit London, Stratford-upon-Avon and the Lake District. It would help when he talked to the women he was trying to con. Most of them loved poetry. Shakespeare, Wordsworth, Tennyson and Kipling. After his visit, with the photographs he planned to take, he could tell them he would be buying a house in one of those areas. They were so gullible, and it would make it far easier to fool them into handing over large sums of money. In fact, right now, as he looked at his screen, he could see the profile of a mature lady. He had made notes of her interests and had started typing them into Google for research. Another day meant another lonely old sucker to reel in.

THIRTY-FIVE

2018

It had been five years since Ashley had changed her name to Grace Springfield. She had done it to honour Roger, the man who had changed her life, and four years since she had left Cupids Arrow Dating.

In that time, the business she and Roger had started had grown beyond her wildest dreams.

This year, LaterLadies had reached a turnover of one million pounds. The business had gone from being based in a spare bedroom, with Grace as the only employee, to a small suite of offices with a staff of five.

LaterLadies is an online dating agency for "*Ladies of a certain age looking for men with manners. Gentlemen who know how to treat a woman.*"

From the start, Grace decided to make the dating website very exclusive. She had decided to charge a premium price for a premium service. And some clients were happy to fork out ninety-nine pounds a month. Other online dating agencies charged less than half this amount. With only eight hundred and fifty members, the business had a million pounds a year income. This year, the company enjoyed the top rating on review sites, with an overall score of 9.9 out of 10. With a strict operating system in place and the help of an outstanding team of ladies, Grace was happy.

Sitting back in her executive office chair, she briefly thought about Ivy, the lady she had worked for and who had been such an inspiration. Thinking of her brought a smile to Grace's face. She was sure that Ivy would be proud of what she had achieved.

Yes, after everything she had gone through over the years, she was finally enjoying the good life.

THIRTY-SIX

2018

Roger came home to find Grace sitting on the sofa, surrounded by travel brochures.

"Are you planning a holiday then?"

"Oh, you caught me. No, not exactly. I happen to know that next month, a certain someone will be celebrating his sixtieth birthday, and I wanted to treat him to a special break."

"Sixty. Wow. The way you say it makes him sound old. Do we know anyone that age?"

"We do. And I want to make it special for him. So please sit down, look through these, and tell me where you want to go. Or do you have somewhere special in mind?"

"Well. I've always wanted to visit Switzerland. I'd especially like to visit Lucerne and Montreux and spend some time relaxing by a lake with a drink in my hand. And they have some wonderful museums."

Roger looked up. He seemed to be visualising himself in the locations already.

"Okay. If that's what you want. I'll get on to the travel agency tomorrow and book it."

"In the meantime, I'll go online and have a look," said Roger.

"I don't much feel like cooking tonight. How about we order a takeaway?"

"Sounds good to me. The usual Chinese?"

"Perfect."

Two weeks later, the tickets for their trip came through, and Roger put them on the dining room table.

Without warning, he felt a sharp pain in his chest. He clutched his ribs in a reflex action and went to sit down on the sofa. As he did, a much more acute pain hit him, and he fell to the floor.

Two hours later, Grace walked in the front door after a long day at work.

She walked through to the lounge and saw Roger lying on his back on the floor. She rushed over.

"Roger!"

She felt his pulse. It was weak. She picked up her phone and dialled 999.

"Ambulance, please. I need an ambulance quickly."

The operator took the details and told Grace that an ambulance would arrive shortly.

Grace was still kneeling beside him. "Hang on, Roger. Please hang on."

It seemed like an age to Grace, but a few minutes later, she heard the siren and rushed to the door to let them in.

Grace went in the ambulance with Roger to the hospital. He was rushed into an inspection area that she wasn't allowed in. She sat in the corridor, waiting for an update.

Three hours later, she was told that Roger was stable but very poorly. He had been transferred to a room in the coronary care unit.

Six hours later, Roger was awake. The doctor told Grace she could go in and see him for a couple of minutes.

She sat by his bed, listening to the heart monitor beep away.

"Well. You certainly gave me a scare. I love you, Roger. Please get better. I don't know what I would do without you."

It was all Roger could do to smile.

"I'll go home and get you some clothes and things. Then I'll pop back later."

She leaned over and kissed him on the forehead.

As she did, the heart monitor changed from a beep to a loud alarm.

As Grace turned around to see what was happening, two nurses rushed in. One of them guided her out of the door.

"Please wait out here. We need the space."

Then, a man in a white coat appeared. Grace assumed he was a doctor.

He rushed in, and one of the nurses pulled down the

blinds so Grace couldn't see what was happening in the room as the response team went to work.

Grace anxiously paced up and down. It seemed like a lifetime before the doctor appeared and pulled down his face mask. "We did everything we could, but I'm afraid he's gone. I am so sorry for your loss."

Grace fell onto a nearby chair, her hands over her face, in fits of tears.

The doctor stood back, allowing her space but hanging around until he was sure she wasn't going to pass out.

As she walked through the front door, Grace had no idea how she'd got home. She couldn't remember a thing since the doctor had given her the shattering news.

All she could think about was Roger. The wonderful man who had taken her in, no questions asked and given her everything she could ever wish for, especially his love. He was gone.

What would she do without him in her life?

THIRTY-SEVEN

2019

It had been a little over a year since Roger had passed away.

For months after the funeral, Grace had barely been able to breathe. It was only by focusing on the business that she had been able to get through the overwhelming grief of losing him.

LaterLadies had continued to grow, and Grace had taken on her sixth member of staff.

Business was extremely good. The level of service Grace offered her clients far exceeded her competitors'. And you couldn't simply join; you had to be approved or recommended. Her success rate was the thing that kept the money rolling in.

Grace had deliberately kept the membership below one thousand. It meant each member could be served better, and the business could find enough men of the right calibre for their female clients.

Grace had never been good at making friends. Without Roger, she felt isolated and alone. Each day just melted into the next. It was the usual routine of going from the office to home. The occasional visit to the supermarket. She'd tried joining a gym, but there wasn't much choice. And the two she'd been to had been a nightmare. The men seemed to think that every woman was looking for a date. After brushing off a bunch of them, she'd heard one telling his mate that she must be, as he put it, "a bloody dyke". After that, she hadn't bothered.

The only positive thing was that the business was expanding. And, with the lease on their current offices coming to an end, Grace had been looking around to rent larger premises. She had narrowed it down to three but hadn't made a final decision.

Susan, her PA, brought in the morning post. One of the letters was from the solicitors handling Roger's affairs.

Grace had been so upset after his death. She hadn't been interested in what he had left her in his will. The letter stated that probate had now been settled. It said they would soon be releasing the funds Roger had left her in his will. It also confirmed the transfer of ownership of the two properties Roger had left her. A large building on the corner of Queensway and Selwyn Street. And the piece of land alongside it. These were plots Roger had purchased more than twenty years ago. Grace called Roger's solicitors and arranged a time to collect a set of keys for the building.

The following day, Grace stood looking up at the building. It was a four-storey property that had originally been the factory and offices of a pottery company. She used the key marked 'entrance door' and inserted it into the lock of the metal-lined door. She turned the key and then grabbed the large pull handle. It took a bit of force, and the door hinges creaked, but slowly, it opened without too much difficulty. Grace stepped inside. There was only a small amount of light, but enough to gain an idea of what it looked like inside. Tomorrow, she would contact the power company and have the electricity put back on. Then, she would call in a structural surveyor to check the condition of the building.

A month later, the surveyor's report arrived in Grace's email inbox. It was good news. The building, overall, was in excellent condition. No structural defects. It seemed it had been built on solid foundations. Even the cellar was well constructed and covered the same area as the other floors.

Ever since she had moved to Trentbridge, Grace had wanted to get into the beauty business. She'd paid a deposit of two thousand pounds for a beauty therapy course but never had the money to pay the balance and take the course. And now she had an idea. The building would be perfect for what she felt Trentbridge lacked. A place where women could meet and get fit. She recalled the gyms that she'd been to. The men who thought they were irresistible. And if she could include a range of beauty treatments and a place where ladies could sit and have a coffee and a meal, it would be perfect. But the main thing she would insist on? No men!

This would be for ladies only. And the more she thought about it, the better the idea formed in her mind. She had even come up with a name for the business.

THIRTY-EIGHT

October 2020

It had taken a little over a year. Finally, the builders were putting the finishing touches to the building. There was only the snagging list to be completed. With the knowledge of helping Roger, Grace knew about snagging and how builders tried taking shortcuts. She had already caught them out on several items, and had made it clear they were not dealing with a "dumb female" who didn't know one end of a gable from the other.

The original refurbishment costs given by the builders had been £329,000. They said this was the lowest possible price. They'd tried to tell her about the problems with the construction. How it would need special materials. But they soon changed their tune when she went through the costs, item by item. It showed them she knew as much about building construction as they did. Suddenly, they were able to reduce the price by thirty thousand pounds. At that point, she knew she was getting a good deal.

All those years of visiting building sites with Roger had paid off. She had picked up a lot of tricks of the trade.

Her list of requirements was comprehensive, and she wouldn't be signing off the work until it was completed to her satisfaction. And that meant the builders wouldn't be paid the final instalment.

Finally, the day came when she was satisfied that all the work was complete, and the builders handed over the keys and the balance was paid. The building was now hers to transform into her dream business. Grace and Fitness.

It was the name she had come up with. Her next task was to register the name as a trade mark.

The removal firm she'd employed had spent the day moving all her furniture from her house into the top-floor penthouse. She planned to rent out the house rather than sell it. One of the items Grace had included in the building construction was a large lift. Luckily, it was big enough for the movers to use. They told her they were extremely grateful. And the fitted furniture company were due to deliver and install the walk-in wardrobe for her apartment tomorrow. They would also feel the same.

For her new business, Grace had done her research well. The demand for yoga and Pilates classes was rising all the time. And the current facilities in Trentbridge were virtually non-existent. A gym was always popular. The facility would be for ladies only. Everything was set for the grand opening date of Saturday, the 5th of December 2020. Her database of mature dating agency clients would come in handy: many lived locally.

Alongside the building, the land had been turned into a private car park. And the bonus: the building was only a three-minute walk from the bus station.

No men allowed. And everything about it was going to be first class. Especially the subscription fees.

The changing rooms were large and luxurious, right down to the toiletries. Everything was branded to represent the name of the Grace and Fitness health centre. The men from the sign company had spent over two hours hoisting the sign into place. Now, the name stood proudly above the exquisitely designed doorway.

The ground floor houses a well-equipped gym, yoga and Pilates studio. It also includes an area for customers to leave their dogs; Grace knew many women were dog lovers and wouldn't want to leave them at home. So, she brought in a specialist to build an area where they would be happy.

On the first floor would be the health and beauty salon. Grace rented the space to a tenant; Sheila Stone had persuaded her husband Andy to spend a fortune putting in the highest-quality fittings. Right down to the lighting. It would undoubtedly give clients the wow factor. It would include tanning booths, a nail bar, an aesthetics studio and a wellness spa.

On the second floor would be the slimming classes, a reflexology studio, a podiatrist and a masseuse. Each of these would be run by small-business owners. They would pay Grace to rent the space. This would create additional income without the need for her to spend anything. It would also house a snacks and coffee lounge, and a vegan café.

The two ladies who ran the catering concessions had just moved in so they could get used to the equipment and make adjustments to the kitchen.

There would also be an area on this floor for offices to oversee Grace's online dating agency. Grace could smell the lovely batches of food they were preparing as she sat in her corner office.

The top floor was a penthouse apartment for Grace. From here, she could oversee her business empire.

Safety was a priority for clients and staff. So all visitors would have to buzz the entry system controlled from the reception desk. The car park was covered by CCTV and powerful spotlights. These were set to turn on automatically when it got dark.

Grace had even been in contact with a local taxi company. The agreement was anyone ordering a taxi would be picked up by a female driver. Yes, Grace was proud to think she had thought of everything.

Strategies for future growth were already in Grace's business plan. These included female boxing lessons and self-defence classes. And once the business became established, she planned to offer it as a franchise. And to launch her own skincare brand using the name "Grace and Fitness".

So far, everything was looking good. Grace believed she had planned everything down to the smallest detail.

THIRTY-NINE

February 2021

Grace looked across her pure white executive desk with its minimal clutter. She gazed into the eyes of the person sitting on the other side. According to her CV, she was the ideal candidate: a highly efficient and reliable person with the perfect qualifications.

Grace had already interviewed seven people. The lady sitting on the opposite side of her desk was the final person applying for the position of bookkeeper and accounts manager.

For her part, Stephanie Waring had undoubtedly made an impression. Partly because she had spent the previous day online and done her research about the company.

The new business, Grace and Fitness, had been open for a little over two months. The membership had far exceeded what Grace had expected. The extra workload was getting too much for her. She had decided the company needed someone full-time to handle the bookkeeping and accounts paperwork.

Grace Springfield looked across at Stephanie.

"Your previous employer certainly speaks highly of you. Mr Madrias says he is sorry to see you leave but understands you are looking for a new challenge. Well, that is certainly something we can offer you here.

"I have a dating agency and, as you can see, I have recently opened this new business, Grace and Fitness. With all the teething problems of starting a new enterprise, the day-to-day challenges pile up quickly. So I will be pleased to have someone of your calibre help me handle the financial side of things."

When it seemed like the meeting was coming to an end, Stephanie asked meekly, "I do have a couple of questions about the role."

She studied her page of notes and questions and looked satisfied with the responses. She already knew the answers from her research, but it always looks good if you ask something. It shows that you're keen.

"I know this is short notice, but I see you've taken your holiday time and left your former employer. So, if you are interested in the position, when would you be available to start?" "It seems like an exciting place to work, and as you say, I've just been on two weeks' holiday, so I'm itching to get back to a normal routine. I could start on Monday if you're happy with everything and you are offering me the job?"

"That would be wonderful and really helpful."

Grace sat back in her chair. It looked like she had found the perfect candidate for this vital position in her company.

FORTY

March 2021

Grace liked to get up early and organise her day before everyone else arrived for work. She sat at her office desk with a cup of her special green tea and switched on her computer. It didn't come on. She walked over to the desk of Susan, her PA, and pressed the ON button on the computer on that desk. Nothing happened. She went into the office of her bookkeeper, Stephanie, and tried her computer – still nothing.

Grace went into the hallway to the utility cupboard, where she knew the central electrical consumer unit was located. She checked every circuit, but they all seemed fine.

Maybe a power cut, she thought. But it can't be. The lights in my apartment are working.

She pulled her mobile from her pocket and called the electrician whose number she kept for emergencies.

"Hi, Peter. It's Grace Springfield. The electrics in the

health studio aren't working. I've checked the units, and they seem okay. Yes, it's fine in my apartment."

"I'm on my way to a job, but I'll swing by. It's not far out of my way. I'll be with you in about twenty minutes."

"Thanks, Peter."

Grace was waiting by the entrance when he arrived and showed him in.

Half an hour later, he walked into Grace's office.

"Very strange. All the units in the box are blown. In all my years, I've never come across that before. The circuit breakers should have kicked in. I've changed them but can't tell you how it happened. It's as if someone changed them all for damaged ones, but of course, that's ridiculous. Why would anyone do a thing like that? But I don't have any other explanation."

"Well, I'm just really thankful you could come over so quickly. The studio has a busy day, and you're a lifesaver."

It had been six days since the incident with the electricity. So far, Grace was no closer to finding out what had happened, and the event was gradually shrinking from her mind.

She was often awake by 5 a.m. and heading to her office before six. As she did most mornings, Grace walked down the stairs from her top-floor apartment. As she walked around, she was trying to savour this new experience. Trying to take in just how far she had come. It was amazing to think what she had accomplished in the past year. Her new business had gone from a building site to a fully functional health and beauty centre. Suddenly, she heard a rustling sound coming from the vegan café. She thought it strange, as no one else would be in the building this early.

Creeping forward as quietly as she could, the sound getting louder as she approached the café counter. Peering over the top, she was alarmed to see two large rats gnawing away at the contents of a plate in the middle of the kitchen prep area. It looked like someone had left a large plate filled with seeds, berries and nuts. Luckily, Grace had a pet rat when she was small, and although shocked at the sight, she didn't scream. Instead, she gently walked backwards and toward her office on the far side of the building. She searched for "Pest Control" on Google and tried five different numbers before someone answered.

"I'm out walking my dog now, but I can be with you within the hour if that is alright?"

Good as his word, Grace received a text message fifty-five minutes later.

Just parking the van. I will be at your front door in two minutes.

Grace had been waiting in reception and at the door before Terry from Sage Pest Control could ring the entry system.

"Thank you for coming so quickly. As I mentioned, there are at least two rats in the café area on the second floor."

Grace led Terry up to the café.

"Fine. It's probably best if you leave me to it. Where will you be if I need you?"

"I'll be downstairs. I've checked the ground and first floors but didn't see anything. But I think I'll check again."

Twenty minutes later, Grace heard Terry coming down the stairs.

"Is there someone who doesn't like you?" he asked.

"What makes you say that?"

"These rats didn't get into the building themselves. These are not wild rats. I found four of them. Don't worry, I can assure you I got all of them. And I didn't use poison, so there will be no problem with the café or food preparation. But it might be worth going over the area and giving it a good clean."

Grace looked at the large square bag Terry had carried in with him.

"Are they all in one of the bags there?"

"Yes. I'll take them away. Don't worry. I assume you didn't spot any others?"

"No, I didn't."

"I don't think they've been here long, probably since last night. It's my guess someone put them here, but I do not know why they would do such a thing other than to make trouble and cause you problems. Call me if you need anything further."

Grace thanked Terry and let him out the front door.

She picked up her mobile and called her cleaner, who only lived a few minutes away.

"Hello, Zofia, it's Grace. Could you come in and do a couple of hours extra this morning?"

"I come now if that okay with you?" she replied in her broken English.

"That would be wonderful, Zofia."

Five minutes later, Zofia arrived. The two women went up to the café and thoroughly cleaned the entire area. They had just finished as the two ladies who ran the café arrived.

Grace thought it best not to mention what had really happened.

"Something had spilled over, so I thought we'd clean it up. I hope that's okay?"

Grace could understand why the two ladies looked a little puzzled.

But they said it was fine and started to unload the four large bags of items they had brought with them.

Grace returned to her office. She wasn't sure what was going on, but it was beginning to worry her. These things were no accident.

Someone was out to make her life hell, as if she hadn't been through enough.

Was it possible someone wanted to ruin her business, reputation and life, and they were prepared to stop at nothing? What sort of person would do that, and why?

But far more important, what would happen next? What if things started to escalate? Would someone end up getting hurt?

FORTY-ONE

March 2021

It had been two weeks since the problem with the electricity supply and a week since the rats. Grace had virtually forgotten about it. She had initially given the matter some thought, but was still no closer to figuring out who was responsible or the reason behind it.

It was 7 a.m., and she was in her office when Zofia, the cleaner, rushed in.

"Miss Grace. The water she is all over the floor. Quick. Quick."

And with that, she turned briefly, looking to ensure Grace followed her.

Zofia led Grace down the stairs to the ground floor and into the changing rooms. When she opened the door, Grace saw the floor was an inch deep in water.

"I see, and I come to you," said Zofia.

Grace could hear running water. She walked through to

the washroom and saw one of the taps was running. Someone had stuffed some cloth in the plughole of the sink, so the water was pouring onto the floor. She turned off the tap.

"It not me, Miss Grace. I not do it." Zofia's face showed the fear of being sacked from a job she enjoyed.

"No, don't worry, Zofia. I understand it's not your fault." Grace could see the genuine concern on her cleaner's face.

Together, Grace and Zofia started to mop up the water, and using the mop bucket, they emptied it into one of the toilets. They were still clearing the water when Fiona Rawlings, the health centre receptionist, arrived for work.

"Have we got a burst pipe?" she asked when she saw the pair emptying the water.

"No, someone decided to flood the changing rooms."

"What? Who on earth would do such a thing?"

"I don't know at the moment, but that's not my main concern. Please call Paulo Rebelo, tell him we've got a problem, and see when he can get here. Tell him it's affecting the business, and I'd be grateful if he could make it a priority."

Fiona went to reception and found his mobile number in the company's office manual.

The plumber told her he was tied up until around lunchtime and would get over as soon as possible.

Paulo liked Grace. Unlike many of his commercial clients, she had paid his invoices in full and on time. And he was impressed with her knowledge of the building trade. He had seen her tell off a couple of his fellow tradespeople who were not doing a high-quality job. As a proud tradesman with twenty-one years of experience, he always tried to do a first-rate job. He was aware a lot of people in the building trade attempted to cut corners. Grace seemed to know her stuff, and as the construction had taken shape, she was there, and she knew what she wanted, and she was going to get it. He admired that. He would finish his current job and then phone the next client expecting him and tell them he was running an hour late. Should be enough time to fit in the work, he thought.

Fiona explained there had been a leak to the clients as they arrived. Luckily, the floor was almost dry when the first clients arrived. It didn't seem to interrupt the classes.

Paulo arrived at 1.35 p.m. and set straight to work, checking everything was in order. He then set up two specialist heaters to help dry out the floor.

"If what you say is true, then this was deliberate," he told Grace.

"Yes. I thought it was. No other problems you can find?"

"Not that I can see. Luckily, you went for the more expensive flooring and sealed it. That's stopped the problem from being a disaster. Everything should be fine once the heaters have dried it out for twenty-four hours. I'll come back tomorrow and check."

Zofia was happy to work the extra hours. The money would come in handy. She had other cleaning jobs, but this one paid the most for the hours she worked. And the equipment was brand new. It made her job much easier. She thought about the tight-fisted clients who expected her to do a good job but didn't want to pay for a decent mop or quality cleaning materials. Yet they still expected their places to sparkle like new.

FORTY-TWO

April 2021

Grace was sitting in her office looking at plans for the next phase of her new business when the internal phone line rang.

"Hello, Grace. Sorry to disturb you, but there is a journalist on the phone, and she insists on speaking with you."

"That's alright, Susan. Put her through."

Susan was Grace's PA, one of the six ladies employed to run the dating agency. Four of the team were responsible for checking the credentials of the men who joined the agency. This was the area where most of the problems could occur. Men who lied about their details or were married and only after one thing.

That was alright if the ladies were aware and consented. Most ladies were looking for a long-term loving relationship or a close male friendship. But as long as they were aware of the situation and consented, what they did was up to them.

The other two team members dealt with the ladies and new enquiries, of which there were many on a daily basis. It wasn't enough that everything was run on an ethical basis. It needed to be seen that everything was above board.

"This is Grace Springfield. How can I help you?"

"Hello, Miss Springfield. My name is Tabatha Watkins. I'm a reporter with the Daily Mail. We're running a story about online dating romance scams. Several of your clients have contacted us, who say they have been scammed out of large sums of money from people they have met online via your website. I wonder if you would like to comment so we can get your side of the story."

"Well, I don't know where you are getting your information from. I can assure you that we have had no reports from any of our members about this. I know other websites have had problems, but I can assure you that we have robust systems in place. We have never, and I stress the word, never had anyone report a problem. It's something I take very seriously because I witnessed such a thing when I worked for another online dating company several years ago. But that has no connection whatsoever with LaterLadies.

"From the very first day I started the business, I have always made sure our clients are aware of these romance scams. In fact, as part of the signing-up process, we produced a video to remind them what can happen.

"We give them the examples of ladies who have fallen for this scam in the past. One of them, called Carolyn Woods, was swindled out of £850,000 by a conman in 2012.

"She was a highly intelligent woman, but the man behind it was so convincing that she fell for his lies. And that's just one of the things we do.

"So, as you can see, we have stringent guidelines to protect our clients from this sort of thing. We constantly monitor our members to ensure we stay on top of anything suspicious.

"So, can I ask who has given you this false information about my company?"

"I'm afraid I cannot divulge my sources."

"Then I would suggest you go back and check with them because, as I have already stated, we have not had a single report of any breaches of our rules. It's something we pride ourselves on. It's why we are rated as the top online dating agency by all of the review sites."

The conversation continued for twenty minutes. Grace was happy to cover all the points the journalist raised. She answered them honestly and with as much detail as she could.

The following day, the phone started ringing with clients wishing to cancel their subscriptions. The newspaper article targeted LaterLadies and made it appear like the website had a problem.

The reporter mentioned that Grace worked for a company with a problem and cleverly worded the article to link it to LaterLadies.

She did this by mentioning that much of the information had come from an "insider". Now, Grace was wondering who within her organisation might be responsible and why they would do it. Such talk would undoubtedly be very bad for business. It could have a significant impact on the future.

FORTY-THREE

April 2021

As Grace pondered over why all of these things were happening, she wasn't aware that in the office next door, her bookkeeper Stephanie was tucking into a bag of crisps with a smile spread across her face – not from the flavour of her snack but from the satisfaction of the damaging false information she had given to the newspaper reporter. That should keep her boss busy while she tries to implement her plans.

During her interview for the bookkeeper position, Stephanie Waring came across as the perfect candidate.

But appearances can be deceptive.

In reality, beneath her outer skin lurks a human snake.

Stephanie has the ability to wriggle out of almost anything. She would slither her way into a position of trust and crush anyone who got in her way.

Any company unfortunate enough to employ her would regret it. She would squeeze the life out of them and gobble up their profits, just as she had done many times before.

She didn't care that three of the places where she'd previously worked had had to close down. A total of sixty-two people had lost their jobs and income. Because she had stolen so much money from the company accounts, it had left them insolvent.

Like the cold-blooded creature she was, she would take everything possible and cause as much havoc as she could. Then, move on to the next company and repeat her underhand activities until that company was squeezed dry.

For this interview, her previous employer, Mr Madrias, had given Stephanie an exemplary reference, but not because she'd deserved it. She'd been careless, and he'd discovered she had stolen money from his company. Before he'd caught her, she had embezzled £38,000 by setting up fake invoices for suppliers who hadn't existed.

It hadn't looked good for Stephanie. He'd been on the verge of calling the police.

But she had an ace up her sleeve. He hadn't realised she was still in the office covering her tracks late one night. It meant she had seen what he did with his secretary when they'd thought everyone else had gone home. She'd shown him the photos taken on her phone.

In exchange for her not informing his wife about the affair and Stephanie leaving the company, he had agreed not to involve the police.

Now, she was eyeing up her next victim. She was out to grab everything she could.

And woe betide anyone who got in her way.

FORTY-FOUR

April 2021

It was two o'clock, and Grace was in her office. Stephanie knocked and walked in. She told Grace that she wasn't feeling very well. Grace had said she should go home and rest and come back when she felt better.

Grace opened the browser on her computer, and typed in "private security near me". When it didn't produce the desired results, she tried "private investigators near me". She then opened a new tab, typed in "local private detectives", and looked at all the results. The top four were ads, and the companies looked to be located in other parts of the country but using a local number, which would then be transferred. Scrolling down, she came across "Phil Jones Private Investigations". This one stated it was the leading company based in Trentbridge. She picked up her mobile and called the number.

It rang five times before someone answered.

"Hello. James Sheldon."

"Oh, hello. I'm not sure if you can help. I seem to have a problem. I suspect someone is deliberately trying to ruin my business."

"That's not very nice. Perhaps you could start by giving me your name?"

"Yes. My name is Grace Springfield."

Then Grace explained about her business and what had been happening.

"Okay, Grace. I suggest we meet, and you can give me all the details, and I can see what I can do to sort it out."

"Thank you. It would be a relief to talk it over with someone."

After Grace explained the beauty centre was for females only, James suggested that he would rather stand out. He proposed they meet at the Albion Hotel, five minutes from the gym.

"So, when would you like to meet up?"

"The sooner, the better, as far as I'm concerned."

"In that case, would this evening be too soon? Say nine o'clock?"

"The hotel has a meeting room. We can use that and discuss things without anyone knowing what is happening."

"Okay. I look forward to seeing you then. I'll meet you at reception."

James asked Grace to email him some details so he would have a chance to go over them before they met.

Grace arrived at the Albion for her appointment with private investigator James Sheldon.

It looked like a very upmarket hotel. It should do. The

front of the hotel had recently undergone an extensive refurbishment. It was the final stage of a three-million-pound upgrade since James had bought the hotel four and a half years ago.

After James had been made homeless, he'd found a spot behind the Albion Hotel where he could sleep. A couple of the staff had looked after him and helped him. Shortly after that, the hotel was put up for sale, and it looked like a developer would convert it into apartments, and the staff would lose their jobs. So James had used some of the £168 million he had won on Lotto and bought the hotel so the staff could keep their jobs. It had proven to be a good investment.

As she walked in, James was standing by reception.

"Hello, are you Grace?"

"Yes, that's right. Mr Sheldon?"

"Yes. Nice to meet you. Please call me James. Let's go through to the meeting room, and we can discuss your situation without being disturbed."

James led her into a room with a table in the centre large enough for eight people to sit around.

"Please have a seat. Would you like tea, coffee or a cold drink, water perhaps?"

"Water is fine. Thank you."

James brought over two glasses of water and sat down next to Grace. He took a sip from his glass before leaning forward, his elbows on the table.

"Let me give you a brief background.

"My business partner, Phil Jones, and I are both ex-police detectives. We have a lot of experience. And so you understand, anything you tell us is strictly confidential. I am here to help you.

"Now. You sounded very worried on the phone. So,

please start at the beginning and tell me what you think is happening. And, if you have an idea as to who is responsible."

"Well. I recently started a new business called Grace and Fitness. It's on Selwyn Street. Things are going well, but someone is trying to sabotage the business. Over the past few weeks, someone has tried to flood the changing rooms. The electrics were tampered with. One morning, as I came downstairs from my apartment on the top floor, I found rats in the kitchen. I called in a pest control man, who told me they weren't wild rats. Someone had brought them into the building.

"We've also had money and goods go missing. Someone contacted the Health and Safety enforcement officer. They told them the property was unsafe, even though it had just been refurbished.

We also had someone pour paint and oil right outside the entrance. Someone could have tripped over and been badly hurt. Luckily, it was spotted in time. We've also had someone break into members' lockers and steal money."

Grace took a pause. She put her head in her hands for a moment, then looked up again as she let out a breath.

"I'm worried that things might escalate and someone ends up getting hurt.

"As well as the effect it's having on the business, I'm concerned for the security of my staff and members of our health centre. And I'm spending all my time and effort thinking about what will happen next. I should be concentrating on the future of the business. It's a new business that seems jinxed from the start."

James looked at her, concerned about what he had heard.

"No, I wouldn't say that. This is down to either a staff

member or a client. As you mentioned to me earlier, as you don't have any male staff or members, we can eliminate half the population. This is someone inside who knows the layout of the building.

"It definitely sounds like someone is out to get you. I assume you don't have any idea who is behind it?"

"No. I've tried to think, but nothing comes to mind. We've only been open for five months, and all our clients seem really happy with our facilities and service."

"How about a rival? As you say, you've only been open for a few months. Have you taken clients away from another business?"

"No. That's the thing. What we offer has very little in the way of competition in Trentbridge. That's why I started it. Because I could see the potential."

"Hmmm. Very strange. I assume you don't have cameras and CCTV in the building?"

"The centre is for ladies only, and many of them will be in various stages of undress. I didn't want to be accused of spying on members, so I only installed them to cover the car park."

"We need to obtain proof; the best way is to capture whoever is behind this, in the act. I know it's not what you want, but I would propose we put covert cameras in the areas where you've had problems.

"We have to be aware it could be a member of staff or, for whatever reason, one of the people you rent space to.

"Surely you can't think one of them is involved?"

"It's the ex-detective in me. In the police, we were taught the ABC principle. **A**ssume nothing, **B**elieve nobody and **C**heck everything. Nobody is ruled out until we have proof they are not involved.

"Now, from what you tell me, all these problems have kicked off in the past few weeks?"

"Yes, so it appears."

"I know a security company who could undertake the work. The system will back everything up onto a secure server in the cloud. So you'll be able to check in real-time or playback anything, whenever you want, from any computer and transfer the footage onto a hard drive. No one would have access except you. That way, everything remains secure. Does that sound like something you would be prepared to entertain?"

"Well. Normally, I would say no, but I really need to get to the bottom of this."

"Okay. I suggest we set it up so that we won't put anything into the changing room area. We put cameras on each floor level but hide them so nobody knows they are there. It's not one hundred per cent ethical, but it is legal. However, considering what has been happening, I don't think we can afford to alert anyone. The company will come in late at night to install everything, so no one knows. The software will be hidden on your network. You'll have an access code so that you can review the footage. And you can view it from any computer terminal in the building. How does that sound?"

"I just need to get to the bottom of this. It's causing me sleepless nights. If there's no other way, then I guess it's what I have to do. Okay, please go ahead and organise it.

FORTY-FIVE

April 2021

The following day, Grace was opening her mail at her desk. The first letter looked official. It was a brown envelope marked on the outside with "HM Revenue & Customs". Strange it hadn't gone to Stephanie Waring, the company's bookkeeper.

Upon opening it, Grace found the letter confirming that the VAT office wanted to undertake an inspection. It asked her to contact them to arrange a convenient day and time. It stated the VAT inspection would take place at Grace's offices. Was this the latest "sting" that someone was playing on her?

Grace was confident that everything was in order. Although she had a bookkeeper to handle the accounts, Grace checked them over. She was always meticulous in her paperwork.

But a visit from the VAT inspector was never pleasant. They were there to catch you out and had the power to go through your accounts going back years. The night before the visit, Grace didn't sleep very well.

A week later, on the dot of ten o'clock, as arranged, a gentleman named Andrew Clayman arrived, and his ID showed that he was from HM Customs and Excise. He was short, maybe five foot three, with unwashed hair and a cheap suit. He was obviously a smoker, and from the redness on his face, Grace thought he might be someone who enjoyed the odd drink, maybe more than the odd one.

Grace had set up a desk in a spare office, and all the accounts and records were waiting for him.

After three hours, two cups of coffee and several questions, he knocked and walked into Grace's office.

"I've found a few irregularities in your accounts."

The pretend smile on Grace's face disappeared.

"Oh, don't worry. Some deductible amounts have been missed on the building work you've had carried out. It seems that you are due a rebate of £3,359."

The fake smile was suddenly replaced by a real one.

"Oh, I see. Well, thank you very much."

"When I get back to the office, I'll process the rebate, and it should be with you within the next two weeks. Thank you for the coffee, and I'll bid you good day."

And with that, he was gone.

The items that hadn't been claimed were the ones Grace had asked Stephanie to include in the previous quarter's VAT return. She would need to have a word with her.

FORTY-SIX

May 2021

Stephanie Waring was not happy. Grace had brought her work into question. It appeared the VAT man had found the business was due a rebate of over three thousand pounds. Her job was to check such things, but she hadn't been focusing on her duties. Instead, she'd been spending her time trying to find ways to cause mischief and problems for her boss. Stephanie had hoped to move money into fake supplier accounts. The problem was the level of access she had to the system wouldn't allow her to add new accounts. To do that, she needed authorisation from Grace. The problem for Stephanie was that Grace was so organised, and she'd set a block on the business bank account.

She knew the business had over four hundred thousand pounds in the bank. She had tried all sorts of things to distract Grace – a number of incidents that should have created chaos. But the woman had dealt with each of them and was still running the business with an iron rod. Try as she might, finding ways to drain the company bank account had come to nothing.

This had never happened before. All her previous employers had fallen for her ploy and taken their eye off the ball, allowing her to set up her scams and gradually drain their bank accounts. She'd been able to set up fictitious supplier accounts and then submit fake invoices for services that hadn't existed.

The company would then pay them, and she would transfer the money from the fake businesses' bank account, which she had set up, and enjoy a life of luxury.

Over the years, it was something she had done for the six companies who'd employed her as a bookkeeper.

Two years ago, she'd been found out and taken to court. The building supplies company she'd worked for in Liverpool had noticed a string of invoices from a company they had never heard of. Stephanie, or as she'd called herself back then, Mary, had been unlucky. There had been a query about an invoice that had caused concern when she was away on a two-week luxury cruise. Unknown to her employers, the holiday had been paid for with the money she had stolen.

Rather than wait for her to come back to work, they'd asked their accountants to look into the matter. When it was discovered that the supplier didn't exist, the police were called in, and she'd been caught. At the time, she had worked there for three months yet had already managed to steal over thirty thousand pounds. Yet the judge had given her a suspended sentence. Two weeks later, she'd moved to Trentbridge and changed her name to Stephanie.

Now, as the things she'd tried had failed to work,

Stephanie had a new idea to get Grace out of the way so she could gain control of the bank accounts.

It had started with a simple thought: if only Grace was off ill for a period of time, then she would need someone to pay the wages and suppliers' invoices. And, of course, the person Grace would turn to was the bookkeeper.

So Stephanie had decided that this called for more drastic action.

She'd been online and researched the exact amount of rat poison you needed to make someone ill but not kill them.

Grace liked a particular brand of Japanese green tea, Tencha Mimoto. Luckily, she was the only person in the office who drank it, and it comes in loose-leaf form. So, adding a sprinkle of rat poison, will not be a problem.

According to the article, adding a small dose would give the person taking it nosebleeds and make them suffer extreme fatigue. That should keep her off work. Her plan was, that with Grace out of the office for several days, she would allow Stephanie complete admin control. That would let her set up fake accounts, raise false invoices and get them paid. She knew it wasn't the perfect plan, but it served the bitch right for standing in her way.

If she cleared the bank account, she would have enough money to move to another town or abroad. Then, she could set up a new fake identity, find another trusting company and do the same again.

For the past four days, Stephanie had been adding small doses of rat poison to Grace's green tea.

She had started with a tiny amount and, each day, had

gradually ramped up the dosage. It was working. Grace had been feeling ill for the past two days. She had been too tired to get involved in the day-to-day running of the business and stayed in her apartment.

Stephanie volunteered to visit her each day and see how she was. It allowed her to spike the tin of green tea in Grace's apartment with the rat poison.

She had told Susan that when she last went up to visit Grace, she'd been resting and had given instructions not to be disturbed under any circumstances.

So everyone had gone home thinking Grace was okay.

FORTY-SEVEN

May 2021

James recalled the man he had bumped into on the railway track. The one who had talked him out of killing himself. It had been nearly two years now. What was his name? Oh, yes. Mick Winner. He'd suggested that James get a dog as a companion.

He'd thought it was a good idea and visited a local rescue centre called A Dog for Life, where he'd seen a lot of dogs. But Rufus had stood out, and the pair had bonded from the start.

One of the first things James had done after Rufus came to live with him was find a dog trainer. He'd wanted to make sure that the dog could be kept under control. The trainer had told James he'd made a good choice.

He said that Dalmatians were one of the most intelligent breeds of dogs. Another good thing James had found out was that fully-grown Dalmatians made excellent companions for jogging. That was handy as James had recently started on a regime to get fit.

With each day that went past, James loved having him around. The dog seemed to understand virtually everything James said. They had started going out for walks twice a day. Once for a jogging session and the other for a romp around the nearby fields.

Rufus picked things up quickly. Whenever James said "walkies", Rufus would wag his tail. He would then go and fetch his lead, bring it over to James and allow him to clip it onto his collar.

When they reached their favourite field, James would throw the ball. Then he'd watch Rufus run off to collect it and bring it back, dropping the ball at James's feet for him to throw again. The dog never seemed to tire of it.

James wondered how the man was getting on. He lived in one of the houses on Asbury Park. He hoped he was happy living there. He made a mental note to check up on him in the near future.

FORTY-EIGHT

May 2021

Now that the hidden cameras had been installed, James had tried to call Grace several times to see if there were any updates. But each time, her PA, Susan, had told him that she was ill. It had now been five days, and she'd told him the symptoms, and he was beginning to suspect something wasn't right.

As an ex-police detective, this was something he had come across before. And with all the problems Grace had been having recently, he was worried this was an escalation of the events.

He had sent several messages to Grace's phone telling her he was worried and that she needed to contact him however bad she was feeling. He'd said she needed to go to A & E. He had offered to drive her and stay with her.

But, so far, he'd had no reply, and he was becoming increasingly concerned about her.

The following day, having heard nothing, he was now getting extremely concerned.

He waited until the evening, but when he called again and got no reply, he decided to drive over and check if she was alright.

He pressed the intercom button several times with no reply. So he keyed in the access code programmed in for the company who had come to install the camera system. The door opened. He called out, but there was no reply. He checked on each floor until he reached Grace's apartment.

As he entered the lounge, he found her slumped across the sofa. She was unconscious. He checked her breathing and pulse. Both were shallow.

He scooped her up in his arms, carried her down the stairs to his car, placed her in the passenger seat, put on her seat belt, and drove straight to A&E at the hospital.

He carried her in, still unconscious, and explained what he believed was happening.

The doctors started to treat her. James told them he would wait.

Two hours later, she was admitted to a hospital ward, weak but conscious. They would keep her in for observation. The doctor said it would take a few days to flush the poison out of her system.

FORTY-NINE

14th May 2021

Grace was feeling much better. She phoned the office, spoke to Stephanie, and explained what happened.

"They think I've eaten something poisonous. But I'm feeling better, so they are going to discharge me in a few days. I will know more after the doctor has done his final tests at seven o'clock tonight," she said.

And finally. There was good news for Stephanie.

Grace had been so ill she couldn't get any work done. So she told Stephanie the password for the administration-level access to the company's accounts software.

Stephanie was over the moon. It meant she could start to set up fake supplier accounts. Then, in a few days, she could begin to transfer money into her bank account. It shouldn't take her long to grab a large part, if not all of it.

After everything that Grace had put her through, Stephanie was beaming. "Don't worry about us. Everyone is rallying together here. Nothing to concern yourself with. You concentrate on getting better, and we'll see you in a few days."

"Thanks, Stephanie. I knew I could rely on you."

At seven o'clock, the doctor was on his rounds. He reached Grace, and after a quick examination, he decided she had made a good recovery. She was well enough to go home tonight. They probably needed the bed for another patient.

She called Stephanie to update her.

"Oh. That's great news. Do you need a lift from the hospital?"

"No thanks, Stephanie. I'll grab a taxi from the rank. Thanks for the offer."

Stephanie put down the phone. She was starting to put things in place but needed a couple more days. She knew if Grace got back tonight, there was a risk that she would start going through the accounts. It wouldn't take her long to discover what was happening: the fake supplier accounts she'd added to inflate the wage bill. And Grace would find the fraudulent letter she'd sent to the bank. The one instructing them she would be transferring a large sum of money to a new account. And at the bottom of the letter, she had forged Grace's signature. So, she desperately needed to ensure her boss didn't return home tonight. She knew that Grace didn't have any family. She could deal with the staff in the office. So once Grace was out of the way, there wouldn't be anyone to stop her.

After speaking with Stephanie, Grace called James to update him, thank him for everything, and let him know she was being discharged. When she did, he insisted on coming to collect her.

At seven-thirty, they were walking down to the main entrance.

"You stay here and rest. I'll go and fetch the car. Give me a few minutes, and then I'll meet you on the other side of the road. It's a no-parking area, but it should be okay if I only stop for a few seconds."

Two minutes later, Grace got a text message.

"Due to the zig-zag lines for the crossing, the closest I can get is a little way down on the other side, to your left."

Grace walked out of the main entrance. She could see James's car parked about forty feet away on the opposite side. She started walking over the pedestrian crossing.

Halfway across, she saw powerful car headlights coming directly at her. Grace stood frozen to the spot.

Two seconds away. The car was going so fast she doubted even being this close to the hospital would save her.

So this was how her life would end. She closed her eyes.

The car was about to impact when two arms grabbed her around the waist and pulled her to the side of the road. She could feel pain. She was still alive.

Someone had made a rugby tackle dive, pulling her out of the vehicle's path just in time. She fell on top of the person who had saved her and looked down. It was James. His lightning-fast action had saved her life.

"I was walking to meet you and saw the car aim at you and accelerate."

Grace looked down at him lying on the ground. He was

crying like a baby. He must have been hurt. Did the car strike him?

Suddenly, there was a loud crash. The car that had tried to run Grace over had collided with another vehicle. James got up, and the pair walked to the spot where the two vehicles were mashed into each other.

Grace stared through the windshield at the immobilised driver, who was slumped over the wheel of the car. Grace gasped as she realised, she knew the driver and clumsily reached back for James's hand, her breaths shallow. He squeezed it, a reassurance she needed right now.

Because Grace recognised the driver. It was her bookkeeper. She couldn't believe that Stephanie Waring had just tried to kill her.

FIFTY

The police arrived outside the hospital and arrested Stephanie. James helped Grace into his car and drove her back to her apartment. They would visit the police station the following day to give their statements.

As James held open the front door to the health centre for Grace, her mobile rang.

"Hello," she answered weakly.

"Hello, Miss Springfield. This is Detective Inspector Eden Gold. We've just started interviewing Stephanie Waring. She's confessed to putting rat poison into the green tea in your office and apartment. I've sent an officer to collect them for evidence, but in the meantime, I want to caution you not to touch them."

"Oh, goodness. That explains a lot. Yes, of course. I'll wait for someone to collect them. Thank you for letting me know."

Grace turned and told James the gist of the conversation.

"Will you stay until they come?" she asked. "I have to

admit, after everything that's happened, I'm a little afraid to be here on my own."

"Yes, of course I will. Look. I've got a suggestion. After they've gone, rather than staying here on your own, why don't you come and stay with me for a couple of days? I've got a spare room. You're welcome until you feel ready to return. I live alone." He could sense she was a little hesitant. "Or, if you prefer, I can arrange for you to have a room at the Albion."

"How can you arrange that?"

"Oh, I happen to know the owner quite well."

James made no mention of the fact that *he* was the owner.

"I think it would be best if I stay at the hotel if that's alright with you."

"Yes, of course. I'll call and arrange it."

It was now nearly nine o'clock. The reception staff would have gone home, but James knew who to call.

He found the number for George Leeman, the night porter.

"Hello, George. It's James Sheldon. How are you?"

"Hello, Mr Sheldon. I'm extremely well, thank you. And yourself?"

"Yes, not bad. George, the reason I'm calling. I'm coming over with a lady who needs a room for a few days. Can you find out which rooms are available and make sure one is ready, please?"

"Yes, Mr Sheldon. I'll make sure everything is in order for when you get here."

"Thanks, George."

Just then, there was the sound of a buzzer.

Grace and James had been waiting in reception. She

went over to the front door and let the officer in.

"Hello. I'm PC Rachel Nason. DI Eden Gold sent me to collect some items for evidence."

The three got into the lift and went up to Grace's apartment. She showed Rachel where the items were and watched as she put on blue gloves and placed the packets of green tea into individual evidence bags. They walked down to the floor below and into the office kitchen. Luckily, Grace was the only person who liked the green tea.

Once she had everything, James took the officer down to the front door.

"Thank you, sir. The detective in charge will be in touch.

"Thank you, Rachel."

While James was showing the PC out, Grace was putting together a selection of clothes and items she would need. She walked through from the bedroom and put the suitcase down next to the lift.

Grace went into her kitchen and threw all of the packets of tea, coffee and items that weren't sealed into the waste bin, just to be on the safe side. She thought of Stephanie. Another person she had trusted had proven to be deceitful.

The lift arrived. James stepped out.

"Have you got everything?"

"Yes, I'm ready."

James drove her to the Albion.

As they walked into reception, George Leeman was waiting.

"Hello, Mr Sheldon. Everything is ready. It's room 103."

"Thanks, George. That's great."

James showed Grace up to the room.

"Wow. It's lovely. Who did the interior design?" enquired Grace.

"I had ... er, the hotel had an interior design company do it, I think."

Grace said nothing but caught what he had started to say. There was obviously more to this man than she realised.

"Well. I'll say goodnight and leave you. George is the night porter and is here all night if you need anything. And, of course, you've got my number."

"Thank you for everything. Especially for saving my life at the hospital."

James said nothing. He smiled and gently closed the door, then made his way downstairs and found the night porter.

"George. Her name is Grace Springfield. She's experienced some trauma and needs to rest. If you could tell whoever is on reception in the morning about Grace staying for a few days and get them to bill everything to my account."

"With pleasure, Mr Sheldon."

James went to his car and drove home.

He noted the date on the dashboard clock. A tear ran down his cheek.

FIFTY-ONE

It was eight o'clock when the alarm on her phone started to beep. It took a moment for Grace to remember where she was.

The bed had been extremely comfortable, and she had slept soundly.

The plan was to go down and have a light breakfast, then call James to arrange a visit to the police station.

"Hi, James. I've just had a nice breakfast. I'm ready whenever you are."

"Okay, Grace. I've spoken with the detective in charge of the case. He can see us at ten o'clock. So, if I pick you up at nine-forty, that should give us ample time."

"Sounds good. I'll see you then."

The police interview with James lasted thirty minutes. Walking out of the interview suite, he saw Grace still being interviewed in the suite next door. He sat down and waited, chatting with a couple of old colleagues as they happened to walk past.

After an hour, Grace emerged from the room, followed by DI Eden Gold.

Grace rushed to James. "They are going to charge Stephanie with attempted murder. And charges of attempted embezzlement. I'll get on to my bank and check everything, then change my passwords. And they say they are considering other charges regarding money stolen from her former employers. She's also confessed to causing the damage at the health centre over the past few weeks. I thought I was jinxed, but she was behind all the problems. They've said they will keep me informed. In the meantime, they will be keeping her in custody."

James had a quiet word with Eden and thanked him for looking after Grace. Then, the pair made their way outside to James's car.

"Right," said James. "Where would you like me to drop you off?"

"At the beauty centre, please. I need to concentrate on work. And bring my team up to date with events."

"Okay. The room is booked for as long as you need it, so take your time."

"Once again, thank you, James, for everything."

He smiled. "Right. I'll drop you off, then I have to get home. Rufus will be wondering where I am!"

"Oh. Who's that?"

"He's my dog. A Dalmatian. And he needs a lot of exercise. He keeps me on my toes, but he's so affectionate."

"He sounds great. I'd love to meet him sometime."

"And I'm sure he'd love to meet you."

James pulled up at the health centre. Grace got out. "Thanks, James. Speak soon.

"And we need to sort out your bill for the work you've done and for arranging the room at the Albion."

"We'll discuss it at some point, but don't give that a thought for now."

Grace went in and up to her office. She needed to tell everyone about Stephanie and what she had been up to. They would all be shocked. She had appeared so nice. Another person who wasn't as they seemed. Could she ever be able to trust anyone?

FIFTY-TWO

It had been a week since Stephanie had attempted to kill her, and Grace was feeling much better. After her mind had kept worrying about the situation, she swapped to a brand of green tea that came vacuum-packed, just for peace of mind.

James had visited her every day, and the pair had spent hours chatting.

She had asked him if he had suffered any injuries. When he replied that he had been fine, she innocently asked why he had cried.

He explained how his family had been killed in a hit-and-run, and although he hadn't been with them, he had felt responsible for not being able to save them.

"And I thought I'd had it bad," she remarked. "Do you want to talk about it?"

"Not right now. Perhaps soon, but right now, I'm looking to the future. Both of my businesses are doing well, so I shouldn't complain. In fact, I've got a company coming to make a promotional video for social media. I've got plans to build it into a brand and, in a year or so, to offer it as a franchise."

"You're certainly ambitious. I can see you achieving whatever you set your mind to."

"Yes. I want to build the business up so that I can sell it when I'm fifty and afford to retire. So, unless I win the Lotto, I'll keep working and hoping things work out."

James could tell it was a random remark, and she didn't know about his big win.

"How about you, James? You must have plans for the future. Or do you make a lot of money being a private detective? Do you make a lot from telling wives their husbands have been cheating on them?"

"Me? I guess I'm happy as I am. Money doesn't mean that much to me. I like helping people. And it's not all about cheating husbands. Sometimes, it's about finding a missing cat."

They both laughed.

What he hadn't told her was that the date he had saved her was the sixth anniversary of their deaths. He also didn't tell her, how, after their funerals, it had caused him to turn to drink and how he had ended up homeless. And he made no mention of the Lotto win or the setting up of his charity. Nor about buying the Albion Hotel to save the jobs of the people who had helped him and given him somewhere to sleep.

Just then, the buzzer on James's phone went off.

He silenced it. "That's my reminder. Time to take Rufus for a walk. I don't suppose you'd like to join us? We go to a field close to where I live."

"Yeah. Okay. Why not," replied Grace, almost surprised with herself that she had agreed to it.

Half an hour later, Grace found herself throwing the ball for Rufus to fetch. James stood to the side, enjoying the sights of both Rufus and Grace having a great time and her looking the happiest he had seen her so far.

After spending half an hour trying to tire out Rufus ... and failing, Grace accepted the offer of a cup of tea at James's house.

"Please grab a seat. I have green tea. It's Twinings. Is that okay?"

"Yes, that's fine. Do you drink it then?"

"No. After I found out that's what you drink, I bought some and tried it, but it's not for me. So, I guess you'd be helping me out if you have a few cups. Otherwise, it will probably stay in the cupboard for months."

Grace laughed.

"Perhaps you should keep it in case you have another visitor who enjoys green tea. A lot of women do."

"To be honest, I think you're the first woman who's been in the house since I moved in."

"Oh, come on. Surely, you must have had some lady friends. You're single, after all, and as a private detective, I bet you have lots of interesting stories to tell. The women must be lining up."

"I haven't dated or seen anyone since my wife. I've found it hard. I'd never imagined life without her. How about you? An attractive woman who runs two highly successful businesses."

James read her body language. It told him something was wrong. "Oh, I'm sorry. I can see I've hit a nerve. I didn't mean to pry."

Grace thought for a second.

"Can I be honest?" She continued without expecting a reply. "I really like you, James. If things were different, then I would like to think that there might be something between us. But I have secrets about my past that would put anyone off. Things I'm not proud of."

"From what I've come to see, you are a good person. There's nothing you can tell me that would make me think less of you. If you want to tell me, I'm a good listener."

Grace sighed. She thought this way, at least it would be out in the open.

"Okay, here goes. I was born in Rotherham, and my name was Ashley McDonald.

"When I was thirteen, I ran away from a care home. I became involved with what has become known as the Rotherham grooming gangs. I was held against my will in a house for over a year. Repeatedly raped and abused. Men coming to the house and using me for sex. Usually four or five a night. I managed to escape and caught a train to Trentbridge, and by a stroke of luck, I ended up living with a man called Roger Springfield and his daughter, Trinny. He became like a father to me. If I had been under eighteen, he would have adopted me. So, instead, I changed my surname to his and started using my middle name.

"He was such a genuine and lovely man. He died a couple of years ago, and I miss him every single day. He's the one who helped me get my first business off the ground. I'll be eternally grateful to him.

"With everything that happened, I find it extremely hard

to trust anyone, and who would want me after my history? Nobody in their right mind would touch me with a bargepole."

Grace sat with her head bowed, not saying a word.

A few seconds passed.

"First of all. You have nothing to be ashamed of. What happened to you was not your fault. And as for what you said about nobody in their right mind being interested in you. Would you consider someone who isn't in their right mind?

"Someone who has attempted suicide more times than he cares to remember. Someone with no friends because he pushes them all away. Someone who doesn't give a flying fig about your past because he can see what a lovely person you are. Someone who only wants to cuddle and isn't sure if they would ever want to take things further. Because they still miss their wife but would like to finally move on, if possible. Do you think you might be interested in such a mixed-up nutcase?"

Grace looked up.

"You mean you?"

"Unless you know any other mixed-up nutcases?"

James moved over to sit next to Grace. He opened his arms, and she fell into them. He held her gently, and for the first time in years, both felt the warmth of another body touching theirs.

Rufus, who had been sitting in the corner, lifted his ears, got up, wandered into the utility room next to the kitchen and lay down in his bed. He would give them some privacy.

FIFTY-THREE

It had been two months since that first evening with James. They were both taking things slowly. There had been more cuddles and a few kisses but nothing more.

They had been out for meals together, and slowly, they were both learning to release their emotions. They were both taking things slow. One day at a time.

Today, Grace was concentrating on promoting her business, Grace and Fitness. She had engaged the services of a local video production company. They were here to produce a short film to help promote the health centre.

A crew of six people arrived at nine o'clock: a cameraman, a soundman, a lighting man, a producer, and a make-up artist. There was also someone they called the runner. It seemed his job was to be at the beck and call of the other crew members. Going out for coffee, setting up equipment and doing all the odd jobs. When the crew arrived, they had spoken with Fiona, the receptionist. Grace had given her the responsibility of showing them around and giving them access to the various parts of the centre.

Grace had already spent a day with the film producer, going over what she wanted them to cover. This had been followed up with a detailed outline. The company then presented a step-by-step storyboard of how the video would look for her approval.

It all looked very professional, and she had given the go-ahead.

They had started with the outside of the building and the car park, showing how secure everything was.

Fiona explained that the safety of clients was a priority. So all visitors had to buzz the entry system controlled from the reception desk. For the safety of guests and staff, the entire car park was covered by CCTV and powerful spotlights that turned on automatically when it got dark. She went on to say they used a local minicab company. The agreement was that clients would only be picked up by a female driver.

Then they headed into the reception area, then into the gym, the yoga and Pilates studio, the area for slimming classes and the changing rooms. They finished filming in the pet hotel, a place where clients could leave their dogs. Fiona explained this was so clients could go off and enjoy the facilities, knowing their four-legged companions were being well looked after. Then, it was up to the first floor and into the top-of-the-range health and beauty salon. As the producer interviewed Sheila Stone, the cameraman moved around, so it looked like they were shooting the film from various angles. There were shots of Sheila walking through each section: the tanning booths, nail bar, eyebrow treatments, the aesthetic clinic, and the wellness spa.

The filming then moved to the second floor and into the two catering areas. The producer interviewed Esme, who ran the coffee shop offering light snacks, and Pandora, who ran the vegan café.

The final part of the filming had been arranged to briefly mention Grace's other business, LaterLadies. The company had their offices on the second floor.

As the film crew made their way into the main office, Grace watched as they set up all of their equipment.

When Grace had asked her PA, Susan, if she wanted to be the face of LaterLadies and appear on camera, she jumped at the chance.

Grace had decided she didn't want to be part of the film. She preferred to remain in the background.

She watched with interest as the producer did the interview with Susan. She felt proud of how she talked about the business and presented the strong points. And Susan looked good in front of the camera. She seemed very natural. Grace watched as the sound man held the boom arm with the microphone steady just above Susan's head but out of camera shot. She watched the cameraman set up one camera in a fixed position and then use a second one to move around to get views from different angles.

Then, as he reloaded a new SD card into the camera, something unsettled her. Maybe it was the way she had rushed down her lunch? She couldn't put her finger on it, but whatever it was, it made her feel uncomfortable and, for some reason, very miserable.

Five minutes later, the crew had finished and were collecting all of the camera equipment and sound and light gear. Grace watched as they packed all of the equipment away.

The producer came over to her.

"You've certainly got an incredible business here, and the team of people have been extremely accommodating.

"We've got everything we need. We'll do the post-production work and send you a finished sample to see if you like everything."

"Thank you, Mark. I look forward to viewing the finished result."

Just then, the runner turned to Mark. "We've got everything ready to go, boss."

As he was about to walk out the door, Mark turned to Grace. "It should take about two weeks. I'll let you know closer to the time."

And then they were gone.

Grace went up to her apartment and made herself a green tea, then sat down to try and work out what had made her feel so strange. She still couldn't put her finger on it, but whatever it was, it made her shiver to her core.

FIFTY-FOUR

Grace was in her apartment, relaxing. It had been a busy day. Membership of the centre was continuing to grow. She had thought about finding a replacement for Stephanie, but the very thought made her put off the decision.

She was half listening to the ten o'clock TV news. As she got up to take the dishes into the kitchen from the meal she'd enjoyed earlier, something she heard stopped her in her tracks.

She listened intently to the newsreader.

The bodies of two young women have been discovered buried in a wood on the outskirts of Rotherham. Police say they estimate they have been there for about twenty years. They have been identified as Joanna Roberts and Layla Jackson, who were both aged thirteen and living at a children's home when they were last seen. The families have been informed.

Photos of two girls flashed up on the screen. She recognised them instantly.

She recalled the night she'd witnessed Mohammed and his friends murder the two girls and wrap their bodies in plastic. It had been the night before she had finally managed to escape from Mohammed all those years ago.

As she thought back and played the horrifying event over in her mind, she realised why she'd felt so uncomfortable during the commercial shoot. The way the cameraman had walked around the office capturing Susan from different angles. That was precisely what Hamza had done as they'd murdered Joanna and Layla. He'd walked around capturing every despicable thing they'd been subjected to.

Connecting the two, she recalled the small tape she noticed in one of the camera cases that the video production company had had. It looked a lot like the tape she'd found inside the money belt from Mohammed's safe. The thought came into her mind. Why would he have locked it in the safe? What could possibly be on it that had been so important?

She was sure she still had it somewhere in her possessions. The boxes of stuff from her house were stacked up in the second bedroom. She'd never got around to sorting them out. She remembered the Nokia phone. It had some phone numbers stored on it. But after twenty years, they were probably useless now. Oh yes, and there'd been the two keys and a credit card. She had never tried to use the card. She didn't have the PIN number, and using it might have alerted Mohammed to where she was. Even though it had been over twenty years, she was still frightened, even by the mention of his name.

She had kept the items more out of curiosity than

anything. But now she was wondering if the tape might have been from the camcorder that she'd seen Hamza using.

Until she'd seen the tape in the video production company's case, she'd thought it was from a Dictaphone machine. Like the ones Ivy had used to tape the meetings when she'd first joined My Friend Wants a Date. But now she recalled the video man from the production company. He had something like it in his bag. It had caught her eye. Could what she had taken from the safe be a videotape? Could it include something that would incriminate Mohammed?

She went into her spare bedroom and started looking through the boxes. Finally, she found the money belt.

But when she opened it, instead of the things she'd expected to find, there was a bundle of fifty-pound notes. She counted them. Four hundred and fifty pounds. Then she remembered. It was the five hundred pounds that Roger had given her, less the fifty-pound note she'd gone back and given to the girl on Price Street. Along with the note that she'd torn in half.

Damn!

If only she'd kept the tape.

She put all of the items back into the boxes. She would go through them again when she was more in the mood.

She noticed a box marked "curtains". Maybe they might fit the window in that room. She'd been meaning to put some up since she moved in, but had never got around to it. As she tipped the contents onto the bed, sitting on the top were the items from the money belt. They must have been at the bottom of the box. She couldn't even remember putting them there. But right in front of her eyes was the small plastic box with the tape inside.

She opened the case and looked at the tape. It had words on the side: Mini DV Digital Video Cassette.

If Mohammed had thought it important enough to put it in his safe, then maybe there was something on it that might prove what had happened that night.

If there was any chance of getting justice for Joanna and Layla, she must do whatever it took. Even if it meant going back to Rotherham and facing Mohammed. Though, even the thought of doing that made her shiver.

FIFTY-FIVE

Grace watched the latest TV news programme. Now that the bodies had been discovered, people might believe her. And was Mohammed still alive? After all, it had been over twenty years.

She hadn't thought about him for a long time. The memories of what that man had done. How many young girls' lives must have been destroyed by that man? She was one of the lucky ones. Thanks to a wonderful man called Roger. And maybe, just maybe, she had the chance of a happy future and someone to share it with.

She needed to find a device to play the tape on. Could the video contain evidence that would help to give Joanna and Layla some long-overdue justice?

She recalled seeing the camcorder sitting in the corner of the lounge the morning after Mohammed and YoYo had killed the girls. She looked at the tape. What could she do with it? It certainly wouldn't fit into any device she currently had. Nowadays, it's all about SD cards.

The next morning, Grace went online and looked at the websites of local camera shops. She didn't find what she was looking for, so picked up the phone. The first shop was abrupt and told her they didn't have anything. At the next shop, the phone was answered by someone who sounded like an older man. He advised her that looking on eBay was the best place to find an old video camera. He gave her the names of a couple of camera models to look out for. She thanked him for his help and opened a new tab on her computer, went on to eBay and typed in the names of the models the man had suggested. There was one being offered in full working condition.

Panasonic NV-GS140 Camcorder 3CCD Mini DV Digital Tape Video Camera. Full working order. £140.

She pressed the **Buy It Now** button.

Grace was sitting at her office desk, her phone rang. It was Fiona from reception.

"Hello, Grace. A package has just arrived for you. Shall I bring it up?"

"No, that's fine, Fiona. I'll come down and collect it."

After going down to the ground floor and spending a couple of minutes chatting with Fiona, Grace went up to her apartment and unwrapped the parcel. Inside was the camcorder. It was in good condition and had all the cables. She read the instruction manual, then plugged it into the mains socket.

She cautiously opened the compartment on the side of the camera and slotted in the tape. The machine made some whirring noises, then went silent and showed it was ready. She flipped out the screen, pressed the PLAY button. The camera whirred again, and the tape started.

Grace recoiled as the face of Mohammed Khan appeared on the screen. For a microsecond, she imagined he was talking to her. Then she realised he was speaking to the person holding the camera.

"Did you get it all?"

Then she heard another voice she recognised. Hamza.

"Yeah. It's great. When you choked her, I zoomed in close. You'll be able to see every detail."

The camera panned around, and all the people in the room came into view. Grace recognised all of them. At some point during her time at Mohammed's house, she had been abused by every single one of them.

The image on the screen went black. Hamza must have turned off the camera.

She sat on the sofa for a few seconds, trying to calm the fear that had gripped her body from seeing all those disgusting men. It had been twenty years, but the memories of what they had done to her were still fresh.

She rewound the tape until it stopped, then pressed play.

Grace's chest tightened, and her stomach churned as the image changed from black to the room she knew so well. The lounge of Mohammed's house in Bramwell Street in Rotherham.

She lifted a hand to her mouth as she watched Joanna being undressed by one of the men. A sob escaped as she watched the men line up and start to have sex with her, forming a sick sort of queue. It brought back memories she had tried to forget over the years. Tears were soaking her cheeks as the camera moved to Layla being subjected to the same treatment.

Grace sat and watched as each line of men took his turn. She didn't want to watch. Even the thought made her feel sick, but she felt obliged to see what happened.

As she watched the final demise of the two girls, Grace was sobbing. She reached across and grabbed a handful of tissues from the box on the coffee table.

Finally, she witnessed Mohammed looking down on the girl he had just murdered, then smiling to the camera.

Grace sat quietly in her chair with the tears still flooding down her face. All the emotion of that night that she had held back for all these years came tumbling out. It was a good five minutes before she could compose herself.

Hopefully, the evidence from the video would put them all behind bars for life. The only problem was, who could she trust? There had been one or two police officers who seemed to be very friendly with Mohammed back in the day. If she gave the evidence to the wrong person, the videotape could disappear, and her new identity and location could be revealed to the gang. Her life would be in danger.

She thought about the options. Perhaps the best thing would be to send the tape anonymously to the local TV station or the BBC. That way, she wouldn't need to reveal herself or get involved.

Grace jumped as her phone rang.

"Hello, Grace." It was Susan, her PA. "Is there anything you want me to do before I leave for the day?"

"Er. No, Susan. I'll see you tomorrow."

"Well, okay. Goodnight."

"Yes, goodnight."

Grace pressed rewind on the camera and waited. Once it

had clicked back to zero, she took it out of the machine and placed it into a drawer.

She poured herself a large glass of wine. It took a while as her hands were shaking. Eventually, the glass was half full. She sat down and took a large swig.

FIFTY-SIX

Grace wanted to help and bring some justice to Joanna and Layla. Equally, she knew that Mohammed was probably responsible for the death of several other girls over the years. This could be just the start of things. Did she really want to put herself through all of the shitstorms that would happen as a result of putting her head above the parapet after all this time?

Perhaps tomorrow, the media will have more details. It was best to sleep on it and see what they had to say.

As she lay in bed asleep, the nightmares returned. After all this time, they seemed so real. Visions of her trapped inside the house and all the disgusting men treating her like a piece of meat. Using her for their own pleasure. She could smell them. Those disgusting excuses for human beings. And supposed to be all religious and God-fearing. Most of them with wives and children. If only the men's families knew what they had got up to. But then again, women were treated as second-class, so they didn't have a say in the matter. According to the conversations Grace had had with the men, all women were good for was cooking, cleaning and sex.

Having not slept well, Grace got up an hour later than usual. She made herself a coffee and sat down to watch the TV news in the hope of seeing if they revealed more about the discovery of the two bodies in Rotherham.

Police in Rotherham have issued an appeal to anyone who might have information regarding the discovery of two bodies buried in Wickersley Wood. Rotherham Police will be holding a news conference at midday and have promised to reveal more details.

Grace phoned downstairs to her PA.

"Morning, Susan. I've got some paperwork to catch up with. I'll be tied up until lunchtime."

"That's fine, Grace. There's nothing urgent in the schedule that I can't deal with. I'll see you later."

The hours until the lunchtime news seemed very slow to Grace. She was used to working at a fast pace. Always busy getting things done.

Finally, she heard the intro music of the TV News show.

Police have revealed more details about the bodies of two young women found in Rotherham. Let's go over to their news conference.

The TV showed a high-ranking police officer in uniform. The caption underneath showed his name as Chief Superintendent Raymond Hargreaves.

> *Two weeks ago, workmen discovered the remains of two bodies buried in Wickersley Wood. Forensic analysis has confirmed these are the remains of two females.*
>
> *DNA results have revealed that the bodies have been there between twenty and twenty-five years. And items found confirm they are Joanna Roberts and Layla Jackson. Their families have been informed. Both girls were thirteen when they were last seen. They had been staying at the Sandbach Road children's home when they disappeared.*
>
> *Police are appealing for anyone with information to contact them. They have set up a special hotline number for anyone who thinks they can help. The number is shown at the bottom of your screen.*

FIFTY-SEVEN

By the following day, Grace still hadn't made a final decision. She would think about it for the rest of the day. But deep inside, she knew that she owed it to Joanna and Layla to help bring the people responsible for their deaths to justice.

The video showed clear evidence of what Mohammed and his friends had done. They were guilty of murder and should be punished. Many times in the past, Grace had doubted that anyone would believe what she had gone through. But now, with the video, there might finally be a chance of the truth being revealed.

Grace watched the six o'clock TV news. There was a rerun of the news conference they had shown at lunchtime. She noted down the phone number that the police officer in charge gave out.

Grace picked up her phone and dialled the number.

"Rotherham Police murder enquiry hotline."

"Hello. I have some information regarding the murder of Joanna Roberts and Layla Jackson. I want to speak with the detective in charge, please."

She waited, and after a minute, she heard a voice. "Putting you through now."

"Hello, this is DCI Barry Yeoman. I was told you have some information for us."

Grace hesitated. Was she making a mistake? But if she was to get justice, she needed to tell someone. The police officer on TV had seemed trustworthy.

"My name is, er, Grace Springfield. Twenty years ago, I lived in Rotherham. My name then was Ashley McDonald. I was living against my will at the house of Mohammed Khan on Bramwell Street.

"I managed to escape. And I took some things from the house. One was a videotape I hadn't looked at until a couple of days ago. It clearly shows the murder of Joanna and Layla in the lounge by several men, including Mohammed. The whole thing was caught on video by Hamza, one of his brothers."

"I see. If that's the case, I would certainly be interested in obtaining that tape. Where is it at the moment?"

"I have it in my possession. I now live in Trentbridge. I can take it to the local police station if you want me to."

"No. They are not involved in this case. So, I would prefer one of my officers to collect the tape. We can't afford for it to get into the wrong hands. This is a very serious investigation."

"I want to make sure and get justice for Joanna and Layla. Can you assure me that will happen?"

The police officer continued.

"I understand your reluctance. I have a daughter the

same age as when the girls went missing. So, I'm anxious to get to the bottom of this case. To show people they can't get away with things like this.

"It could be that you are still suffering from the trauma of what you went through. We can arrange to get you counselling to help. Tell me. Have you ever spoken with anyone about this?"

Grace felt more reassured. He sounded like he wanted to help.

"No, I haven't spoken to anyone. Until I came across the tape, I didn't know how to prove anything."

"I understand. So, tell me again, how did you manage to get hold of the tape?"

"When I escaped from the house, I grabbed some things from Mohammed's safe. Until I saw the news, I had forgotten all about it. I didn't even know it was a videotape. It wasn't something I really wanted to recall, but then I thought about Joanna and Layla. So I watched it, and that's when I saw what they did."

"Listen to me, Grace. We need to get that tape so that we can find the people responsible. Do you want to help me get justice for these two poor girls?"

"Yes, of course I do."

"Then I really need to get that tape as soon as possible. I'm going to send two of my best men. I will get them to leave right now. They should be with you in about two hours. Please have the tape ready. They will need to take a statement from you. Will you be there when they arrive?"

"Yes, of course."

"Good. Remember, I'm on your side. We're doing this together. For the two girls. Is that what you want?"

"Yes, of course."

"That's wonderful, Grace. And thank you for contacting us."

Grace put down the phone. The detective had sounded really nice. She was reassured that something would be done. At last, Mohammed and his friends would finally see the inside of a prison and, hopefully, would never be let out. She looked down and noticed her hands were trembling.

She glanced at her phone. It was ten past six. They would arrive at around eight.

Grace felt hungry. With everything that had been happening, she hadn't eaten all day. She went downstairs to the café on the second floor run by Pandora. They were open until seven.

She ordered a vegan jacket potato.

Sitting down with a cup of green tea and waiting for the food, she noticed Sheila Stone at the counter.

After ordering her food, Sheila looked around, and when she saw Grace, she wandered over.

"Mind if I sit with you?"

"No, of course not, Sheila. I've been meaning to catch up with you. How's it going?"

"It's going great. If business keeps increasing like this, I might have to take on someone else."

"That's good to know. The membership is going well, so I see no reason why you can't expect more clients. I've certainly heard some good reports about your treatments. The lady you have offering nail treatments always seems to be busy."

"Yes. I'm just grabbing a quick snack while I can. I have a client booked in for eight tonight."

Grace looked up as Pandora appeared holding her baked potato.

"Mmmm," said Sheila. "That smells good. I wish I had ordered that, but I opted for a salad. I need to keep a check on my weight. My divorce should be through soon, and then Chris and I hope to get married as soon as possible."

Sheila was married to a detective, DCI Andy Stone, but she had met a man at work who was twelve years her junior. He'd persuaded her to go for a drink, and things had developed, and eventually, he had won her over. She had heard about Grace wanting someone to set up a beauty salon in the health centre and persuaded her husband to pay a small fortune to set it up. At the time, he'd needed to make it appear like his marriage was solid to help him gain a promotion. In return for Sheila going along with it, he'd agreed to pay for everything. Sheila was only two years older than Grace. When they met, they had got on well. They were very similar in looks and what they wanted from life. To be independent and be a success in their respective fields.

After chatting as she enjoyed her meal, Grace finished and went upstairs to her apartment. She glanced at her watch. The time was approaching seven o'clock. She found an envelope and Sharpie and wrote the name DCI Yeoman on the front and placed the videotape inside.

She glanced at her watch. The police officers would be here in about forty-five minutes. If they wanted her to give a statement, it would be after nine by the time they left. She decided to take a quick shower.

At five minutes to eight, Grace went down to reception with the tape in the envelope to wait for them. She saw Sheila sitting there.

"Hi, Sheila."

"Oh, hi, Grace. I'm just waiting for my eight o'clock client. She's bringing her dog. I told her we have an area where she can leave him."

"I'm expecting visitors as well. Two men. They should be here shortly."

Grace put the envelope on the counter. Then her phone rang. It was James.

His voice was soft. "Sorry to call, but I couldn't help it. I've been thinking about you all day."

"Can you hang on a second?" Grace preferred to chat in private.

"Sheila. I'm just popping upstairs. I'll be down again in a couple of minutes. If the two men arrive, can you let them in, please?"

"Not a problem, Grace. My client just sent a text to say she's running a few minutes late. And I have a couple of messages to send."

As Grace walked into her apartment, she smiled as she lifted the phone to her ear.

"I've been thinking about you too. And Rufus."

"Say hello to Grace, Rufus." She heard the dog give two short barks. She laughed.

The pair chatted away like a couple of lovesick teenagers.

FIFTY-EIGHT

The intercom for the front door of Grace and Fitness buzzed. Sheila walked behind the reception desk and pressed to open the door. Two men walked in. Sheila was busy replying to a text message. She looked up and noticed the envelope that Grace had left on the counter.

"Hello," she said, holding up the package and seeing the name written on it. "You must be DCI Yeoman. I assume this is what you've come for?"

One of the men walked over and took the envelope.

Sheila's attention was focused on the text message. So she wasn't paying attention.

"Thank you. And we'd like you to accompany us."

"Er, what? No, you don't understand. I'm—"

The two men grabbed hold of Sheila. One of them from behind. The other stepped forward and placed a strip of gaffer tape across her mouth. Then he put a blanket over her head. They bundled her to the front door and out to their car. Sheila was thrown into the back, her mobile fell from her hand and slipped under the seat in front. One man got in beside her and the other into the driver's seat. The vehicle sped off.

Grace finished her call with James and walked down to reception. She looked around. At first, she thought Sheila must have returned to the beauty salon, but then she noticed the envelope was gone. She walked back up to the beauty salon and called out to Sheila. No reply. She called out again as she walked from room to room, then hurried back downstairs, a fear rising in her mind as she did.

She rushed into the reception office and over to the computer, keyed in the password and brought up the program the security company had installed. She found the camera for reception and pressed the playback for the past ten minutes. The image came up. She adjusted it to play at four times the normal speed. Then watched in horror as what had happened to Sheila became clear. She dialled James and told him what had happened.

"I need to make a call. Make sure the front door is secure and wait for my call."

Three minutes later, her mobile rang.

"I'm on my way over to you. I've just called Andy, Sheila's husband. He's tracked her phone and sent officers to intercept them. I'll be with you shortly."

A minute later, there was a bang on the front door. "Grace. It's James."

She opened the door.

James rushed in. "Andy says the signal from Sheila's phone shows she's in the Wolfe Street multi-storey car park. I'm going to head over there."

"I'm coming with you. It's my fault. They must have thought she was me."

The pair got into the car, and James drove off. The car park was only a two-minute drive away.

As they turned the corner sharply, Grace heard a rustle from behind her. She turned to see Rufus stretched across the back seat.

On the top level of the Wolfe Street multi-storey car park, one of the men who had grabbed Sheila was on the phone.

"We're here. And we've got the bitch."

"I'll be with you in a second. Just walking up the last few steps."

The back door of the vehicle opened. One of the men who had grabbed Sheila removed the blanket and pulled the gaffer tape away from her mouth.

Sheila looked around, first at the two men on her left, who she'd seen at the health centre. She turned to her right, seeing a man she had never seen before. He smiled. "Remember me, Ashley?"

"I ... I'm Sheila. I don't know who you're talking about. You've got the wrong person."

Mohammed looked at her closely. He narrowed his eyes as he leaned in for a closer look. His face turned from a smile to anger.

"That's not her. You've got the wrong bitch."

The man replied, "But she was there. She had the package. Look." He handed the envelope to Mohammed.

"At least you got something right."

He turned to Sheila. "Start talking. Who are you, and where is Ashley?"

"I don't understand. I don't know anyone called Ashley.

Grace told me that someone was coming to collect a package. She left the envelope on the counter while she went upstairs. Then, these men arrived. I gave them the envelope, and they grabbed me."

"What?" He turned to the two men. "Didn't you ask her fucking name?"

"We ... we thought it must be her. She handed us the package."

"Well. You were wrong, but I've got what I came for. Without the tape, she can't prove a thing. Now, let's dispose of this bitch, whoever she is, and get back home. Throw her over," commanded Mohammed.

"What? No, please, no," Sheila pleaded.

The two men grabbed Sheila and started dragging her toward the car park's edge.

She grabbed hold of one of their arms, trying to get away, but he was too strong. As they got closer to the edge and started to lift her, she could feel the wind whipping around her. She grabbed the wall and clung on. One of the men was prising her fingers away. Just as they were ready to shove her off, they heard a siren, and a police car drove up the ramp, its headlights blinding them. As his heavies froze, caught in the glare from the halogen beams, Mohammed made his escape down the same stairway he'd appeared from.

He'd parked on the floor below. Within seconds, he was in his vehicle. He ducked down as a second police car came rushing past him and continued up the ramp, heading for the floor above.

He started the engine and slowly made his way to the exit, trying to look like he didn't know what was going on.

James drove into Wolfe Street and approached the car park. Grace was in the passenger seat. As they were close to the entrance, she called out.

"It's him! It's him!"

James looked across at her.

"Driving that taxi. It's him. That's Mohammed."

"Are you sure?"

"Trust me. I'll never forget his face for as long as I live."

The taxi sped off. James turned the car around, glancing to check that Rufus was okay on the back seat, then started to follow the taxi, keeping a reasonable distance.

James spoke to his phone. "Call DCI Andy Stone."

"Hi, James. Sheila's safe, thank goodness. And we've got both of them."

"That's great news, Andy. Grace is with me. She recognised someone as we reached the car park. They must have arranged to meet someone else. We're following him. He's heading toward Kingsway. It's a dark blue Skoda Octavia Estate. Can you send someone to, oh hang on, I think he's spotted us. He's just speeded up and it looks like he's heading out of town."

"I'll get some backup over to you."

"Okay, Andy. I'll call with an update in a while."

Five minutes later, James called again. "Hi, Andy. From the look of it, he's heading toward the motorway."

"We've got a problem. Traffic has reported there's just been a massive pile-up on the junction of Baddeley Green Lane. The route to where you are is totally blocked with a lorry on fire. It will be a while before I can get anyone out to you. If you can, keep track of him, and I'll get a patrol car to you just as soon as I can."

It was obvious that Mohammed was well aware he was

being followed. His speed increased, and he started to take more risks, overtaking other vehicles. In a queue at a set of temporary traffic lights, he purposely held back until they changed to red. Then he dashed through in an effort to lose his unwanted tail. Unfortunately, because the road was so busy, Mohammed was stuck behind other vehicles, so it wasn't long before James and Grace were able to catch up to him. Both vehicles were capable of exceeding a hundred miles an hour. James's car was a Ford Mondeo, so both vehicles were evenly matched. There was little chance of Mohammed outrunning them.

FIFTY-NINE

As the chase proceeded, a light rain started to descend. James turned the wipers to intermittent mode.

Mohammed's car was a few yards in front. Every few seconds, he would edge out a little to the right, checking the road ahead. He was waiting to see if there was a possibility of overtaking. But each time, his attempts were thwarted by the volume of oncoming traffic. Had it been a straight road, he might have had a chance, but it was a typical B road with curves and bends every few hundred yards.

Grace looked across at James. He looked relaxed and in control. Suddenly, she felt the car turn sharply. She looked up and noticed Mohammed had turned down a track to the left, and James was following. A hundred yards on, the road became more like a dirt track. Mohammed's vehicle was throwing up a dust trail. James slowed down as the visibility decreased. It was pitch black, and James was driving by headlights.

Up ahead, there was a large burst of dust. James slowed down. As it cleared, Grace saw that Mohammed's car had struck a stone wall right next to a sign saying "Tanners Viaduct".

A small amount of smoke was coming from under the bonnet of the Skoda. The driver's door was open, but there was no sign of Mohammed.

The wall was between two paths. One forty-five degrees to the left, the other forty-five degrees to the right. James and Grace got out. Apart from the slight rumble of traffic in the distance, there was silence.

"Have you got your phone?" asked James.

"Yes."

"Okay. Call 999 and tell them where we are. Get them to send a couple of cars. Tell them I'm an ex-detective.

"I'm going to look for Mohammed. I'll try this way first. Stay here. Don't move. Keep the doors locked and call me if you see him."

James took the track to the right. Within a few seconds, he was out of sight.

Grace pressed 999 on her phone and relayed the message. After being transferred to another operator, she was told they would arrive in ten minutes.

She sat on the passenger seat with her legs swung out the door. Suddenly, she heard a sound coming from somewhere down the path to the left.

She listened and heard it again. A rustling sound.

She got up and started slowly walking down the path. After a few yards, she found herself on the viaduct with a thick stone wall about three feet high on either side. She walked on, then heard the rustling sound again, coming from over the wall to her left. She leaned over and listened. Nothing. She looked down at the ground, probably a hundred feet below. Still she couldn't hear anything. Then, a hand grabbed her from behind and whipped her around.

"Well, well. Fancy meeting you here," quipped Mohammed.

Grace stood glued to the spot. Petrified. A small escape of urine ran down her leg.

Before she could react, Mohammed grabbed her and put his hands around her neck.

"I should have put you out of your misery years ago."

He pushed her, and she fell, landing with her back across the twelve-inch-wide wall.

As he towered over her, pressing down on her neck, her left hand felt a loose rock. She brought it up to the side of Mohammed's head with as much force as she could muster. He fell to the ground. It took Grace a few seconds to recover, then get to her feet and make a run for it.

Just as she did, Mohammed grabbed her foot and swung her around. She spun, falling over the wall's edge but grabbing the thin ledge with both hands. Her legs swung over the edge into thin air, and she was hanging on for dear life. Mohammed laughed as he climbed up onto the top of the wall.

"Time for you to disappear again, Ashley. Oh, I forgot. You call yourself Grace nowadays."

Mohammed looked down at Grace as she desperately tried to cling to the wall with both hands. He smiled as he brought his foot down to stamp on Grace's left hand. Her body twisted slightly as she was left clinging on to the brick-work with just one hand.

Mohammed smiled as he leaned over the edge.

"I think it's time for you to say goodbye." He smirked.

"You'll never get away with this," shouted Grace.

"Oh. I think I will. Well, I can't hang around all day, Ashley. Nice to see you again, but now it's time to say goodbye."

He laughed again, raising his foot to bring it down on her right hand.

As he did, he heard a loud growling sound behind him. He turned to be confronted by a fierce-looking dog snarling at him with its teeth snapping. The animal lunged forward. As Mohammed turned to try and fend off the animal, he lost his balance. He fell backwards, over the edge of the wall, just missing taking Grace with him by millimetres as he plummeted to the rocks a hundred feet below. His petrified voice crying out, "HELLLPPP!" Then silence.

The feeling gradually returned in Grace's left hand, and she managed to grab the ledge just as James appeared out of the darkness. He bent down to grab her arms and help pull her up. "Hold on," he said as he hauled her to safety.

He pulled her away from the wall, and the pair hugged.

"Phew. That was close. I thought I was done for until Rufus turned up." She put out her arm, and the dog rushed over. She gave him a good, solid hug.

"What a good boy. So brave."

The dog wagged his tail as she patted his head.

"How did he get out?" asked James.

"I think I must have left my door open when I heard a sound and came to investigate."

In the distance, they heard the sirens of police cars. They started walking back toward the car hand in hand, then James put his arm around her shoulder, and she snuggled up to him. Rufus followed closely behind, wagging his tail.

The blue lights came into sight, with the wail of sirens growing louder. Relief began to creep in, but the gravity of everything that had just happened hit Grace like a wave. She stopped in her tracks, looking up at James. "There's more, James. You know it's not over yet. Mohammed wasn't working alone."

James's face darkened, his arm slipping away as he turned to face her. "What do you mean?"

Grace whispered, her voice trembling. "The other men involved, and the police officer. I want them all to pay for what they did to Joanna and Layla."

SIXTY

It had been two days since the alarming confrontation with Mohammed.

Grace and James had both attended interviews and given statements. Each of them went through every detail of what had occurred. From the moment Grace had recognised Mohammed as he drove away from the car park until the police turned up at the scene.

James had been told by DCI Andy Stone that they had recovered Mohammed's body. And at the multi-storey car park, they had arrested two suspects who had since been identified as police officers from Rotherham. They had been charged with attempted murder and kidnapping. James was relieved to learn that Sheila was safe and recovering from the ordeal. And the good news was, the videotape had been found in Mohammed's jacket pocket.

The police had told Grace that the person referred to on the tape as YoYo was actually DCI Barry Yeoman. He had been arrested at his home in Rotherham. Grace had been informed that a lot more arrests were planned as a result of the video. She was promised that charges for the people involved in the murders of Joanna and Layla were sure to follow. When it went to court, she would be called as a witness.

SIXTY-ONE

The flight from Murtala Muhammed International Airport landed precisely on time. The gentleman walked out to the limousine he had arranged to take him to his hotel. He was staying at the Park Tower in Knightsbridge for two nights before his planned trip to Stratford-upon-Avon.

After arriving and booking in, the gentleman was escorted up to his room by the hotel porter.

After his long flight, he was tired and decided to retire early. Tomorrow, he planned to visit many of the tourist attractions. Especially the Tower of London.

Following a leisurely breakfast the next morning, he left his hotel intending to visit Westminster Bridge. He wanted to take photos of the place where William Wordsworth was famed for composing many of his works. It would be of interest to the unsuspecting woman he was currently charming out of her life savings. She had just sent him a text message. He was composing a reply as he crossed the road. Looking down at his phone, he looked left to check nothing was coming, then stepped onto the road.

Joseph Okecuku never saw the large bright red Parcelforce lorry that killed him. He'd forgotten that in England, they drive on the opposite side of the road to Nigeria.

SIXTY-TWO

Sheila was back at work, playing down the event by telling her clients that the worst part of her ordeal was the two chipped nails she had suffered.

Strangely, the publicity had resulted in Grace and Fitness attracting new customers. For now, Grace had decided to use her accountants to deal with bookkeeping and accounts work.

There was still a shadow hanging over her and James.

Stephanie Waring had been charged with attempted murder and four charges of fraud. Her trial would be in a few months. Grace knew Stephanie wasn't the type to go down without a fight.

But for now, Grace had other things on her mind. James asked her if she would like to go away for a few days' holiday, and she said yes. When he asked where she would like to go, she surprised him and said Switzerland.

The thought of sharing a few quiet days in the Alps with him stirred something in her.

Roger Springfield had requested to be cremated, and

Grace wanted to take him on the holiday he'd never managed to enjoy. As they locked the door behind them and walked toward the waiting taxi, James took her hand.

She squeezed it, grateful for the warmth and comfort he brought. And a few days in a luxury hotel and a romantic setting with James...

Well, you never know what it might lead to.

TITLES USED IN THE RESEARCH

Broken and Betrayed – Jayne Senior
The true story of the Rotherham abuse scandal
Violated – Sarah Wilson
Easy Meat – Peter McLoughlin
Inside Britain's Grooming Gang Scandal
Girl for Sale – Lara McDonnell
Groomed by a Gang – Christina O'Connor
I Never Gave My Consent – Holly Archer
Prey – Cassie Pike
Secret Slave – Anna Ruston
Stolen Girl – Katie Taylor/Veronica Clark
Survivors – Maggie Oliver
Trafficked – Sophie Hayes

I was recently made aware of another book.

Snatched – Elizabeth Harper

She is a campaigner and public speaker who makes people aware of what happened.

About The Author

My name is Lee Wood, and I write British Crime Thrillers that take you on a rollercoaster ride.

I've always been interested in crime and started reading *Sherlock Holmes* when I was about eight years old.

I even helped the police solve a crime when I was only eleven years old after buying several books on what today would be called forensics.

Apart from writing and reading books, my other passion is music.

I live in Cambridge with my lovely wife, Elizabeth.

You can stay in touch with me via my website
https://leewoodauthor.com

Lee Wood
BRITISH CRIME WRITER

BOOKS IN THE SERIES

Trentbridge Crime Series

Mr Lucky - Book one

Lucky Break - Book two

Dead Lucky - Book three

Thank Your Lucky Stars - Book four

Lucky To Be Dead - Book five

Not Your Lucky Day - Book six

Lucky For Some - Book seven

Die Lucky - Book eight (January 2025)

Next Book in the Series - LUCKY FOR SOME

The next book in the series is waiting for you.
Grab your copy NOW.

A serial killer is on the loose, but with other events taking place, the police could be forgiven for thinking it's not the biggest problem they face. Things are going on that risk the town of Trentbridge sinking into chaos. So why are the police only now finding out about them? It seems like dark forces are at work, trying to take over.
And on top of this, someone is killing old ladies while they sleep in their beds. Can DI Eden Gold and DS Carla Parsons find the killer before they strike again?

Printed in Great Britain
by Amazon

56423405R00165